EIGHT DAYS

JACK BENTON

THE SLIM HARDY MYSTERY SERIES

The Man by the Sea

The Clockmaker's Secret

The Games Keeper

Slow Train

The Angler's Tale

Eight Days

"Eight Days"
Copyright © Jack Benton / Chris Ward 2020

The right of Jack Benton / Chris Ward to be identified as the Author of this Work has been asserted by him in accordance with the Copyright, Designs and Patents Act 1988.

All rights reserved. No part of this publication may be reproduced, stored in a retrieval system, or transmitted, in any form or by any means without the prior written permission of the Author.

This story is a work of fiction and is a product of the Author's imagination. All resemblances to actual locations or to persons living or dead are entirely coincidental.

For Don and Sue
the adventurers

EIGHT DAYS

1

Every day could be a new beginning, Slim thought, as the gate closed behind him, leaving him alone to experience his first breath as a free man in nearly eight months. It was a cold one too; it had been the chilliest winter he could remember, while on top of that, at forty-eight years old he now had a proper criminal record to go with his old suspended one.

Every day could be a new beginning, or the resumption of a shambling past, a ramshackle train hauled out of a siding shed and cajoled down the track for one last calamitous journey.

One or the other, the beaming sun overhead seemed to say. Make your choice. And Slim had. He patted the letter tucked into his coat pocket and started down the street, away from the prison gates, away from his troubles, and away from a reputation left shredded and a business fallen to seed.

Eight months inside had helped with one thing—he was able to walk past three pubs with barely a glance, having finally achieved an extended period of sobriety. But without the booze he felt a void inside, one he needed to fill.

A rope around his neck would do it, severing any pretense at recovery, any vain hope that he could salvage something from the embers of his life. But, as he thought with a wry smile, that would disappoint those types who liked a good scrap, who cheered on the underdog. And one of those types was Slim himself.

At a bus stop at the end of the street he caught a bus into the town centre, and there he boarded a train to Exeter. From Exeter St. Davids he walked up to the bus station and caught a National Express coach to Cornwall.

At ten minutes past six on a rainy Tuesday night in February, he got off the bus at the stop on Westgate Street in Launceston, Cornwall, across the street from a closed hairdressers and an empty chippy, its lights casting a pale glare onto the road outside. As he stood there in the rain watching the bus pull away, an inside light came on in a Ford parked up the street. The driver's window wound down and a balding, middle-aged man leaned out.

'Excuse me, but are you John Hardy?'

Slim lifted a hand as he walked across the street.

'It's nice to meet you,' he said, extending a hand as the man climbed out of the car, an umbrella simultaneously unfolding above the man as though he were an aging butterfly emerging from a cocoon. 'But most people call me Slim.'

'Slim,' the man said, shaking Slim's hand, then leading him around to the passenger side without letting go, perhaps afraid Slim might dissolve into the night. 'Thank you for coming. Georgia could hardly believe it when we got your letter.'

'I still have yours,' Slim said. 'It got me through a dark

time.' He patted his pocket, feeling the crumple of paper inside.

Slim climbed into the car, the man closing the door for him. The interior was clean but smelled of fish n' chips, the hot, oily scent making Slim's stomach grumble.

'Sorry, I couldn't help myself,' the man said, climbing in and shaking the umbrella off at his feet. He nodded at an empty punnet sitting on a protruding cup holder, then swiped it away, stuffing it into a plastic bag. 'A pet craving, I'm afraid. Let's not tell Georgia, shall we? She's prepared something far more exotic.'

Slim shrugged. 'Well, the bus was ten minutes late. I could hardly expect you to starve on my account.'

The man chuckled as though Slim's words had sealed their brotherhood.

'I'm presuming you're James Martin?' Slim said, as the man steered the car away from the curb and gently accelerated up the empty street.

'Yes … I do apologise. I'm afraid I find it hard considering myself a player in all of this. It's all really Georgia's doing. I'm just going along with it, acting as the driver and all that. It was her idea to contact you. I know she has her fears and everything, but you see, I've always considered the mystery solved. After all, Emily came back.'

2

IN HER EARLY FIFTIES, GEORGIA MARTIN HAD A KINDLY appearance which would suit the proprietor of a flower shop or cosy village café. Prematurely grey, she was soft of features, low of stature, and had a warm smile which immediately put Slim at ease.

'You must be starving,' she said by way of greeting, with one hand shooing James into a cloakroom to change out of his coat while waving Slim forward into a snug dining room with the other. All cottage eaves, stone walls and cubby holes containing standing lamps and pretty ornament displays, Slim felt like he'd stepped onto the set of a period drama, the steaming bowl of country stew waiting on a wide hardwood dining room table, accompanied by a bread roll that looked fresh from the oven, only accentuating the effect. He allowed Georgia to usher him into a chair and push cutlery into his hands.

'I know you've had a long journey,' she said. 'Tea? We'll get you settled, then we'll talk.'

She sat down across from him, as though waiting for him to start. A moment later she jumped up again,

Eight Days

tittering, 'James, I forgot to take John's coat. How silly of me.' She flapped a hand in front of her face. 'Goodness, I'm afraid I'm all flustered. I just can't believe you're really here.'

'Please call me Slim,' Slim said, slipping off his coat and handing it to James, who had reappeared just in time. 'Everyone does.'

'Slim ... I like that. Nothing to do with your weight, surely?' She added a fluttery laugh to emphasize the joke.

'It's a long story, but one that would put you to bed early.'

Georgia and James left him alone while he ate, something he found unusual considering how keenly they seemed to have anticipated his arrival. As he listened to the low buzz of the television from behind a door leading to the kitchen, he wondered how his body would cope with such culinary richness after eight months of prison food.

In the end, he had to leave half of it. He called Georgia and James back into the room, then apologised, blaming eight months of calorie counting.

'If you would prefer to get some rest and then talk in the morning, I've already made up the spare room—'

Slim lifted a hand. 'I'm fine to talk now. I don't sleep much.'

'Coffee? Or something stronger?'

Slim smiled. 'Coffee is fine. Black. As strong as you can make it. If you have half a filter left from yesterday, add an extra spoonful of ground then microwave it for two minutes longer than necessary.'

Georgia smiled. 'I'll do what I can.'

She started to turn but James put out a hand. 'You stay and talk to Slim, love,' he said. 'This is your thing after all.'

Was that a scowl which crossed Georgia's face momentarily as James went out? Slim couldn't be sure.

The woman ruffled her skirt and then sat down across the table.

'He no longer cares,' Georgia said. 'After Emily came back and tests showed that—physically at least—she was fine, James wanted to forget about it. I don't blame him, really.'

'But you can't?'

Georgia shook her head. 'I need to know where she went. I won't ever find peace until I know. It's that motherly thing, knowing you let your child down, and needing to fill in the spaces so you can understand where you went wrong.'

Slim leaned forward. 'I understand,' he said. 'I'm sure I'd feel the same if I had children. Now, in your own words, as best you can, tell me what happened.'

3

'June, 2018,' Georgia said. 'I mean, it's nearly two years ago. Most people would have let it go by now. Wouldn't they?'

'That depends on the circumstances,' Slim said, sipping on a coffee that really needed to be left in the filter for a couple more days.

Georgia sighed. She had poured herself a glass of wine at which Slim was trying not to stare.

'Emily was supposed to go to netball club up at the leisure centre after school,' Georgia said, rubbing her eyes. 'We didn't expect her home until seven o'clock. We later found out she'd left school early, after lunch.'

'Any particular reason?'

'She told her best friend, Becky Walsh, that she wasn't feeling well. We only live a mile from the school, and I'm a stay-at-home mum these days, so of course had she done so, I would have seen her.'

'Did the school get in touch with you when she didn't show up to her afternoon classes?'

Georgia looked pained. She squeezed her eyes shut as

though trying to blot out the memory. 'They tried,' she said. 'Someone from the office called twice, but I was out in the garden and we ... we don't have an answer phone.'

Slim frowned. It was something he might need to come back to. Most phones these days came with one as standard, so it would have taken effort and intent to manually disable it.

'So you had no idea she'd gone out of school until she didn't come back from her practice?'

Georgia sighed. 'No. At around eight p.m. we started to call around her friends to see if she had stopped by. At nine we called the leisure centre, who told us she had never been there. After that we immediately called the police.'

'And what happened?'

'They scrambled every officer in North Cornwall. You know what they say about child abductions—that the first hour is vital. We'd already missed it.'

'But they didn't find her?'

Georgia shook her head. Sadly, her hands began to shake as she held the glass, an indication of an affliction Slim knew only too well.

'They had sightings and leads to go on, all dead ends.'

'No suspects?'

'Oh, they had plenty. One of the first people to be investigated was the P.E. teacher from her school who coached the netball club. But that one, like the rest, came to nothing in the end.'

'I'll need a full list if you want me to conduct an investigation.'

Georgia nodded. 'Oh, we have one. A few names that never made the police's radar, too.'

Slim wondered what family feuds he might be set to uncover.

'How long was she gone?'

Eight Days

'Eight days. She disappeared on a Tuesday, and reappeared the following Wednesday. It was the longest eight days of my life.'

'Tell me about how she was found.'

Georgia leaned back in her chair, staring up at the ceiling. She opened her mouth but didn't speak for a long time. Slim was about to ask what was the matter when he realised that he already knew the answer; that everything was the matter, that there was nothing about anything that had happened that could ever be right again.

'Tell me, Georgia,' he said quietly. 'No matter how ridiculous it sounds. Believe me, I've heard enough in my time that I won't discount anything. How was she found?'

Georgia looked at him. Her eyes were filled with tears that dribbled down her cheeks.

'She wasn't,' she said. 'Not really. I don't believe the girl that came home is my daughter.'

'What did the police say?'

'That the girl they found is Emily. She was found in a patch of woodland near Polson, just outside Launceston. She was awake, but she was disoriented, as though she'd only just woken up. When they questioned her later they found she knew basic information such as her age and home town, but she had no memory of events, nor what had befallen her during her disappearance. She was five kilograms lighter, her hair slightly shorter, her skin mildly tanned as though she'd been out in the sun. She had sand between her toes.'

'She suffered some kind of trauma which caused the memory loss?'

'That's what the police said. But there were other things … even when she recognised me, hugged me, kissed me … it didn't feel right. I brought her up. You think I wouldn't know my own daughter?'

'Sometimes a traumatic event such as this can drive a wedge between people,' Slim said. 'The old familiarity takes such a knock that you see everything in a different light. Relationships often struggle to recover.'

'I'm not talking about an affair,' Georgia said. 'I'm talking about the disappearance of my only child.' She stood up, picked up her wine glass and half turned towards the kitchen as though to refill it, then paused.

'You've had a long journey,' Mr. Hardy,' she said. 'I think it would create a clearer picture in your mind if we showed you as much as we could. Emily's staying with her grandmother for a while so we won't have any awkward questions just yet. I've made up a room for you. I'll have James show you up.'

'Thank you.'

As Georgia left to call her husband, Slim tried to read her body language. The excitement he had sensed on arrival had faded, replaced by something like regret.

Was she having second thoughts about contacting him?

4

'It was right in there,' James said, leaning against the car's bonnet, hands clutching a flask of tea. 'I can show you the exact spot if you like, but I thought you might want to have a look for yourself first. It's about fifty yards in, by the grey rock.'

Slim nodded. 'Sure.' James's reluctance was apparent, but he had guessed correctly that Slim would want to go alone. In a case two years old there would be no clues left that the police hadn't already found, but nothing ruined a man's thoughts like the idle chatter of a nervous companion.

A stile led over a stone wall onto a forest path that threaded its way alongside a river. Tall oaks and sycamores rose over a leafy hillside, but the path was well trodden earth with patches of artificially laid gravel where too many tree roots had become exposed.

Slim knew from an ordnance survey map of the region and James's cluttered conversation that the path was a public footpath, and emerged onto another B-road a mile farther along the valley. Despite having no real parking at either end, the path was popular among walkers of more boisterous dogs because of a couple of pretty pools farther up the trail, and close enough to the village of Polson that energetic people could park at the church and walk down.

He spotted the grey rock immediately. It was part of an outcrop where the river made a sharp, gurgling cut back on itself. A large beech had grown over the outcrop, its roots now creating enclaves in the riverbank in which fish could hide.

The river itself was a man's height below the undercut riverbank. The path skirted the grey rock, rising slightly before inclining down towards the level of the river as it arced away out of sight into the trees.

The path was wider here. Significantly, perhaps, an old bench sat back in the undergrowth, almost entirely reclaimed by vines and brambles. From the bench, one could have sat and watched the girl as she lay by the grey rock, in the background a view through the trees to the bottom of a steeply sloping field.

Slim did what he learned in the army, squatting low to the ground and slowly turning in a circle, letting his senses control the flow of information. Not only establishing what he could see from this point, he also gave consideration to what he could hear, how the wind felt on his cheeks, and any unusual smells.

James had claimed on the drive over that the police believed the abductor had pulled up to the stile and carried Emily inside, leaving her by the grey rock before making off, but being here now immediately made the theory seem preposterous. Not only was the grey rock a fair walk in from the stile, but it was completely open, visible from the road. Anyone looking up as they drove past would have caught a glimpse of the girl and rendered the whole endeavor pointless. No, Slim felt certain Emily had been left in this exact spot for a specific reason.

The way the grey rock protruded from beneath the roots of the tree trying to smother it made it look like an antiquated sacrificial altar, some kind of prehistoric symbol. That the girl had been laid down as some sort of sacrifice was fanciful but not impossible; in his years as a private investigator Slim had learned to rule out nothing. It was unlikely, a silly theory, even, but able to be disregarded? No.

It was the kind of place you left a body which you wanted someone to find, but with just enough delay to allow you to get out of range. Emily, of course, had been unconscious but alive. This only reinforced the theory that her death had not been intended.

Why, then, take her in the first place? It wasn't impossible for a kidnapper to have a change of heart, but it was rare. Most abducted either stayed that way, or were found, usually dead.

Slim closed his eyes, listening for anything that sounded out of place. There was the gurgle of the river rushing over rocks, the rustle of leaves in the breeze, and the creak of swaying boughs. In the distance, the sound of a car.

And there, something else, a stronger creak, almost a groan.

Slim stood up. It came from farther down the path.

He followed the trail for fifty metres or so before it opened out at a wide pool. Not deep enough for swimming, with its sandy shore area it would nevertheless have made a decent picnic spot, and a couple of trout the size of Slim's hands darting around in the shallows might have interested youngsters with fishing rods. Nearby was a flat, grassy area which would have caught a summer afternoon sun. The grass was a little worn as though families sometimes came by here. Near to the edge of the river bank was a dirty glass jar lying on its side, the dried remains of some flower stalks still inside.

The creaking came again. Slim looked up.

There, hanging from a protruding branch was the knotted remains of a hunk of rope. Hunk was the only way to describe it, because it looked like multiple ropes had been used over the years to replace those which had frayed, so now the whole tangled mess looked like something the sea might wash up on a beach. What was clear was that it was incomplete; it dangled several metres above the pool, creaking as it swayed in the breeze. To the right the riverbank lifted to make an overhanging ledge, and Slim smiled, feeling momentarily nostalgic.

The remains of an old rope swing, long ago either cut or rotted and fallen. He shrugged, remembering days when he had been young enough to enjoy such a thing. Then, stuffing hands into his pockets, he turned and headed back to the road.

5

With a coffee by his side, Slim pored over a map of the local area in which Emily had been found. He had been unable to see any houses from the spot by the river, but according to the map there were three local properties within half a mile, or within what Slim considered screaming distance. Any farther away and the girl's cries might have been mistaken for the distant call of a bird.

The question of whether she had made any sound or not remained to be examined. He was yet to meet the girl herself either, who would be the best source of information. In the meantime, the better a picture of the crime he could build in his head, the better armoury he would have when the time finally came.

Georgia was pottering in the garden, seemingly content to let Slim investigate the case at his own speed. James was sitting in the living room, watching TV, on-call should Slim request a driver.

Surreptitiously, he had begun to make notes on both of them, too. He could ask them outright, of course, but that would allow the intrusion of bias, assumption, speculation.

There would be time for all that later. For now, Slim wanted hard facts.

A glimpse of James's driver's license had revealed the man to be fifty-six, born in February 1964. Georgia was just a month younger, birth date according to a doctor's letter lying on a tray in a sideboard March 17th. Therefore, Emily had arrived late in their lives.

The average middle-class person's life followed a consistent path of school to sixth form to university to career to marriage to kids. Even a long university course kicked out at twenty-two, and while it was possible James and Georgia had simply worked for fifteen years before getting married—a wedding photograph on a shelf in the living room had a date stamp of July 9th, 2002—the possibility existed that they had done other things in the intervening years. Other journeys, other loves, marriages, heartbreaks. Most abductions were carried out by someone known to the family; if Slim could find a skeleton in the family's closet he would have an automatic suspect.

With a sigh, he folded up the map, slipped it into his bag and then drained the rest of the coffee. Standing up, he called to James that he was going for a walk to clear his head. James offered to accompany him, but again Slim was keen to get a feel for the local area on his own. James sounded relieved when he declined. The volume on the TV rose a couple of notches.

A pleasant spring day welcomed him outside. The road on which the family lived was calmly suburban, a tree-lined avenue called Tavistock Road which connected the centre of town to a large Tesco on the outskirts. At a roundabout in front of the supermarket, Slim had the option to take a road that led up to Launceston College, the secondary school, or across a bridge spanning the A30 bypassing the town to the south. If instead he turned north out of the family property, a winding road led through farmland down to the village of Polson Bridge right on the Cornwall-Devon border, where Emily was found.

Emily had walked to school through a series of alleyways cutting between lines of houses. Of course, like most teenagers, it was unlikely she had ever taken a direct route, going via friends' houses or places of interest or entertainment. In a quiet historical town like Launceston, these consisted of the Tesco, the quiet town square with its small array of shops, and the local leisure centre, situated on the edge of Coronation Park, which topped the town's other main hill, opposite the one on which stood the crumbling ruin of a 13th century castle, the town's main tourist attraction.

Georgia claimed her daughter's abduction had likely taken place along Windmill Hill, which connected the top of Coronation Park with the town centre. It was the quickest route to the shops from Launceston College, a route often used by schoolkids, but with enough cover that someone could have taken her in the middle of the day without being seen.

Slim found himself walking up the steep hill into town, cutting through alleys where he could to get around walking the length of roads that circled the hill, finding himself out of breath as he emerged onto Coronation Park, an innocuous open space of playing fields with just a few scattered trees on the south side. Across the gentle slope he spotted the telltale discolouring of the grass where older trees had been uprooted, as long ago as the terrible storm of 1987, so James had said.

Slim, his body still adjusting to walking for long periods after eight months behind bars, popped into the leisure centre to get a drink from a vending machine. There he paused to look at the schedules pinned to the notice boards. On a poster headed by RESERVED FOR SCHOOL USE ONLY he saw netball listed from 6-8, three nights a week.

It might be worthwhile to talk to the other players about Emily's behavior leading up to the day of her disappearance. Slim knew that kids were often closer to teammates than classmates, although as a private investigator he had no power to force someone to talk. Children tended to clam up when faced with an authority figure, afraid of letting slip something incriminating. Adults, on the other hand, tended to be looser-tongued when they considered themselves in the clear. It was basic human nature to try to push the eyes of suspicion onto someone else.

He was just about to head back outside when a man's voice hailed him from behind.

'All right there, mate? Need any help?'

Slim turned. The man was young, handsome, hair highlighted blond, fit with a tennis player physique. He lifted a hand in a half wave as though to remind Slim who had spoken. A name tag with the leisure center's logo identified him as *Paul*.

'A little too late for me,' Slim said.

'Ah, it's never too late,' Paul said. 'We have classes to suit all ages. What are you, mid-fifties?'

'Forty-eight,' Slim said. Then, with a wink, he added, 'I forgot to brush my hair this morning.'

6

Slim didn't have a computer nor could access the internet on his ancient Nokia, so he walked down through Coronation Park to the local library. A few minutes online was enough to unearth a couple of articles about questionable conduct by the netball coach Dave Brockhill. A P.E. teacher and a thirty-year stalwart of Launceston College, Brockhill had been accused by a girl left unnamed due to legal reasons of inappropriate behaviour, something it took a little more searching to discover amounted to the sending of text and email messages requesting personal information, as well as following her across various social media platforms. It had fallen short of official stalking or sexual misconduct standards, but had been enough for Brockhill to find himself suspended, a period during which, due to the ongoing Emily Martin case, he had decided to take official early retirement.

With a little digging, it wasn't hard for Slim to uncover the man's address. He lived across the valley from Launceston Castle on a housing estate in the neighbouring village of Newport.

For the time being, Slim decided not to pester the man. Instead, now that he had the chance away from the Martins' curious eyes, he searched online for more information about Emily's disappearance. Bypassing the usual media fronts, he headed for the public forums pertaining to unsolved crimes or those with mysterious circumstances.

Such sites were the haunt of crackpot conspiracy theorists and paranoid naysayers, but often clues or ideas leading to other perspectives could be unearthed if one looked carefully. Slim found a couple of recent threads related to the case. One was specifically for offering theories on who had taken Emily, another where people were suggesting reasons for her memory loss.

Opening the latter first, Slim scrolled through several dozen answers. The overwhelming suggestion was that she had been drugged and probably raped. Some users suggested quite graphic levels of sexual sadism which left Slim uncomfortable, and likely said more about the user than their knowledge of the case. According to Georgia, there had been no evidence of sexual assault. If these internet trolls didn't know that, it was unlikely they had much else useful to offer. A few of the more sensible answers, however, suggested names of particular drugs which might cause short- or even long-term memory loss, so Slim jotted them down on a piece of paper to further investigate later. There were other answers of course, of varying degrees of probability, from amnesia induced by shock or blunt trauma, even asphyxiation. Again, Georgia had claimed Emily had no physical injuries.

One theory that Slim kept coming back to, however, was one of the least likely at all.

That she was faking it.

He couldn't believe the girl could hold her act in front

of the police, but maybe it wasn't that complicated. Maybe she hadn't been abducted at all.

Maybe she had run off, intending to disappear just long enough to worry her family. Or perhaps it was a mixture of both. Something had made her lose her memory, but for eight days she had simply wandered, through sheer luck avoiding the efforts made by the police to find her.

Emily was still at her grandmother's house, according to Georgia. The girl would be sixteen now, officially an adult, and able to control her life. That it had been three days and Slim had seen nothing of her suggested a family rift Georgia didn't want to talk about. He had purposely not pursued an interview with the girl, but the time was coming when he would have no choice. He didn't look forward to the prospect. Would he be met with general apathy or an aggressive refusal to talk? After all, perhaps for Emily, as it seemed with James, the matter was now considered closed.

Slim left the library and headed back up to Coronation Park. A number of houses lined the steep road that passed the park's entrance. Slim pulled a clipboard from his bag, opened the cover and drew two lines down a blank sheet of paper. Then, as he walked up the hill, he made a note of each security camera he saw, drawing another line to indicate the direction in which it pointed, and whether it would have viewed the road. Some of the largest properties in town were located here, and most had some kind of security system. On the downside, they also had the biggest hedgerows, and in many cases large farm-style gates which would have obscured the view of the road.

Slim was yet to see what were available of the police reports, and in any case it was too early to begin knocking on doors. Georgia's brief overview claimed that a white transit van of unknown origin had been seen in the days prior to the abduction. The white van had been mentioned by two residents of this street, but had never been tracked down. While it could have belonged to an abductor lying in wait—something so clichéd it made Slim grimace—it was as likely to belong to a delivery driver or contractor, perhaps parked up somewhere quiet to eat lunch while avoiding paid parking.

Coronation Park opened out below him. Slim looked down the wide grassy slope, wondering where his next step lay. Georgia wanted him to interview Emily and then systematically go through the suspects one by one, as though he were a hypnotist who could draw out hitherto repressed or withheld information. In the real world, things didn't work that way. The police were pretty good at their jobs and would have covered most bases. The best Slim could do was find some vital clue which had slipped through the cracks, or try to see everything from a missed angle.

And a good place to start was by covering the background.

He walked to a bench with a view down over the park to the leisure centre at the bottom, and pulled out his phone, dialling a number engrained in his memory.

'Hello?' said a familiar voice.

'Don? It's Slim. How are you?'

Donald Lane, an old platoon mate who now ran a private intelligence service, let out a gasp. 'Slim? Good God. You slipped off the radar for a while, didn't you? Where have you been?'

Sure that along the grapevine of old military voices it was likely Don already knew Slim had done time, Slim chose not to go over ground he'd rather forget.

'Somewhere pretty unpleasant,' he said. 'The good news is that I'm back on the wagon.'

Eight Days

'And bad news for whoever you're after, no doubt. How can I help, Slim?'

'I just need a background check. A couple of fairly innocuous types called James and Georgia Martin.' He gave Don their address. 'I just need to know if there's any obvious dirt for now. Nothing too deep. If anything stands out, please let me know.'

'Right on. Give me a day or so.'

'Thanks.'

Slim hung up. He was still staring at his phone when he became aware of a group of schoolgirls wearing the uniform of Launceston College approaching him. For a moment he wondered if they meant to talk to him, but then they were past, heading up the hill and away down the road which led to the town centre. He checked his watch. 3.45. School had finished shortly before and now the pupils were heading home. Other groups had appeared, cutting through the park in various directions. Almost all of them were in pairs or groups. One solitary girl stood out. Overweight, and limping a little under a bag which looked heavy, she followed a path that led behind the leisure centre. Slim watched her until she was out of sight, then stood up and headed down the hill in the same direction. Aware of a few eyes following him, he made a point of not making eye contact with anyone, even when he heard a muttered insult of 'hobo' come from a group of boys. He had been called far worse, and while the time might come when he needed to talk to local kids, for now he had other avenues to explore.

He had rounded the leisure centre and started down a path that led towards the A30, when he stopped. Someone was crying nearby. He took a few more steps, catching sight of someone through a stand of trees.

The fat girl. She had sat down on a bench just off the

path, facing a small duck pond. Face buried in her hands, she was sobbing uncontrollably.

Slim wanted more than anything to walk on by. He had only been out of prison a few days and was a stranger here. It was better that he flew under the social radar for as long as possible, and he had nothing to gain from involving himself in some bullying issue he had no way to resolve. He started past, but his conscience got the better of him.

He walked off the path, giving the girl a wide berth, then approached her from side on in an attempt to avoid scaring her. She was still sobbing. He walked within a few steps, and was still thinking about what to say when she glanced up and noticed him.

The fear in her eyes stunned him into silence.

'No!' she shrieked, attempting to jump up quicker than her size allowed. Her bag fell off the bench, contents scattering across the grass. She fell to her knees, scrabbling for them at the same time that she turned to Slim and shouted, 'What do you want? Leave me alone!'

7

Slim found his voice at last. 'Wait. Please. I heard you crying, that's all. I wanted to see if you were all right.'

The girl was still reaching for her things, but from her frustrated sighs Slim knew she was close to giving up. He saw now that she had an unattractive brown birthmark down the side of her face from just below her left eye to her jaw. Narrower at the top and bottom, it widened in the middle to almost touch her nose.

He also saw what she was trying to gather from the ground: a cluster of books and magazines which looked brand new.

Reaching for one last magazine, the girl gave up, slapped her hands down on the ground and let out a muted swear word.

'You're having a bad day,' Slim said. 'I'm not likely to make it any better. If you're all right, I'll be on my way.'

He started to back up, but the girl looked up at him, eyes really seeing him for the first time.

'I've got no money, if that's what you want,' she said. 'What are you, homeless?'

Slim glanced down at his clothes. 'You mean the jacket, or the jeans? I'm afraid I just got out of prison. I haven't had time to go shopping yet. Not that I've ever been one for fashion.'

'You just got out of prison?' The girl twisted around and sat up, her eyes suddenly bright with genuine interest. 'Did you kill someone?'

Slim shook his head, remembering what he had been convicted for, and the blood that had been washed off his hands by careful police reporting. It was best to keep his answer vague.

'I caused a bit of damage, then went on the run for a while. I was drinking too much at the time.' Even though, as he remembered it, it had been one of the drier periods of his life. 'I served eight months. It wasn't all bad. I gained some weight, dried out, and even learned to sew.'

'Did you get your arse kicked?'

'In prison?' Slim smiled. 'It wasn't that kind of prison. I played a lot of table tennis and read more books than I've ever read in my life.'

'What was the food like?'

'Bland. I bet you get better school dinners. You're at the secondary school?'

The girl nodded. 'Counting the days until I can leave. I hate every minute of it. I'm not stupid though. If I bunk off as much as I like I'm going nowhere. I might end up like you.'

'I hope not,' Slim said. 'My name's Slim, by the way. It's not my real name, but it's what everyone calls me. I didn't mean to startle you and I didn't mean for you to drop your bag. I guess I'm old-fashioned, that's all. I can't walk past when I hear a young girl crying.'

The girl shrugged. 'It's cool. Most people wouldn't give

Eight Days

a crap. My name's Bernadette.' She tapped the birthmark on the side of her face. 'Or as the pricks at school call me, Burned Bernie. Might as well get it out of the way so you don't have to pretend it's not there. It's a birthmark, and no matter how much people go on about not judging people on appearances and all that, it's made me the class outsider since kids were old enough to take the piss. Believe me, there's nothing you could say that I haven't already heard, and please don't patronise me with the whole "you're no different to anyone else" thing, because we both know I am.'

She gathered up her bag and sat back down on the bench. She didn't invite him to sit, so he lowered himself to the ground, sitting cross-legged, half facing her, half facing the duck pond. He watched a couple of ducks squabble over a piece of bread that had got caught in some reeds for a few seconds, then said, 'Can't you get laser surgery or something these days? I'm no doctor or anything but—'

'No, you're not. Yeah, there's stuff you can do but I'm a minor, aren't I? My parents aren't bothered. Not about me at any rate. The bookies, maybe. Or the pub.'

Slim, who considered the second a disliked former friend whom he could never quite sever ties with, just nodded. He knew enough about the world to know a few kind words would make little difference.

'Did you steal those books?' he said at last. 'I'm not judging you. Believe me, I've done far less time than I deserve.'

The girl's face hardened and Slim sensed a lie coming. Then it softened and she let out a disarmed sigh. 'Yeah. Out of the WHSmith down town. Kid on duty was reading a magazine behind the counter. Didn't even know I was there. So what?'

'It's not a great way to start out in life. Can't you go to the library?' Then, remembering the size of the town library, he said, 'I suppose you could ask them to order in what you want.'

'I sell them,' she said. 'Online. Make a little money. Got to, haven't I?'

'Can't you get a part-time job?'

She tilted her head to reveal the full extent of the birthmark. She had acne too, and a tilt to her eyes that made her appear permanently angry.

'Not many places want me serving beans on bloody toast,' she said. 'You get told at school that we're all equal, but we're not, are we?'

Slim could only sigh. 'No, we're not,' he said at last.

Bernadette smiled. 'Christ, great boost of confidence you are. Felt better before. Don't you have somewhere to go? The JobCentre or a crack house or something?'

Slim shook his head. 'Actually, I'm a private investigator.'

'Yeah, and I'm the queen.'

Slim ignored the sarcasm. 'I'm investigating the disappearance of Emily Martin. Did you know her?'

The natural sneer which Bernadette carried through every expression fell away, replaced by an unsettling blankness.

'Yeah, I knew her,' she said. 'Year above me at school.'

Slim caught something in her words which reminded him of something Georgia had said.

'What do you mean, knew her? You know the police found her, don't you?'

'Yeah,' Bernadette said. 'Not the same, though, was she?'

'Can you think of any reason why not?'

Bernadette shivered even though it's wasn't that cold.

'They say *he* took her, and when he takes you, you don't come back the same and you're not the same ever again.'

'Who are you referring to?'

'The one who scares all the kids. The Woodland Man.' Bernadette chuckled. 'You know, for a moment, when I first saw you, I thought you were him.'

8

Slim wandered the streets for a long time after parting company with Bernadette. It was dark when he returned to the Martins' home. Georgia had set out tea and biscuits for him in a back room she had cleared out for him to use as an office. When he enquired about Emily he was told the girl was still at her grandparents' house.

Insisting that he would meet her soon, Georgia told him to relax, then bustled off into the kitchen to prepare dinner. James, she explained, had gone to visit a friend and wouldn't be back until late.

Waiting until the sounds of cooking from the kitchen ensured Georgia was busy, Slim went out of the office room and made his way up the stairs.

The bathroom was on the right, so he opened the door to allow him to quickly slip inside if Georgia came upstairs, then headed along the landing to Emily's room.

Cracking the door, he found it empty. Curtains were pulled back to reveal a pleasant view of fields, filling the room with light that banished shadows to the corners. A bed stood against one wall, a wardrobe and bookcase

30

against the other. A desk stood just to the side of the window. The decor was pretty, orange floral, the carpet a plain light blue. A handful of books stood on shelves, but nothing seemed out of place, as though Georgia bustled through with her duster and vacuum on a daily basis.

Slim stared, wondering what he was missing. As he figured it out, he almost slapped himself with frustration. It was so obvious.

Nothing personal. No textbooks, knickknacks, pictures of bad selfies taped to mirrors. No posters of pop idols or sports stars. No clothes draped over chairs or shoes thrown into a corner. Were it not for the sign on the door announcing EMILY'S ROOM, Slim could have believed he had made a mistake.

He reached into his pocket for a camera, before realising with frustration he had no such item anymore. Something else to put on expenses, perhaps. Instead, he backed out of the room and headed downstairs, making sure to leave everything as he had found it.

Downstairs, Georgia was still busy in the kitchen, so Slim returned to the office room and jotted down a few notes. He remembered the end of the exchange with Bernadette, aware that in other circumstances it might have made him laugh or shake his head with disbelief.

The Woodland Man. It was a silly local kids' story. Bernadette hadn't had time to elaborate, hurrying off before Slim could grill her for details, but she would be easy to find if he needed more information.

He made a note to check the internet, but he doubted he would find much. Most likely he would get his best information closer to home.

He waited until after dinner. Georgia, in what seemed to be a newly established norm, served him in the office room rather than the dining room. After dinner, he brought his plates to the kitchen and then interrupted while she was washing up.

'Do you have time for a few questions after dinner?'

'Sure. Let me clear these things.'

They sat down with coffee in the living room. Georgia was keen to ask how much progress had been made, but Slim shook his head. 'I'm still building up a picture in my head,' he told her. 'It would be wrong to feed you half-baked ideas. Now, can you tell me a little about Emily's personality? In particular I'm interested in what she might have been afraid of, what she might have disliked.'

Georgia frowned. 'Well, she was never a fan of broccoli.'

Slim resisted the urge to sigh, aware he could be in for a long evening.

'Anything else?'

'Yes, uh, she didn't like the dark. When she was little, we always had to leave her door open, and the light on in the hall.'

'Common among children, I believe,' Slim said. 'Keep going.'

'I'm not sure she really had much she disliked. She was always a happy girl.'

That referral to her daughter in the past tense again. Slim ignored it as he said, 'Any figures or characters she had a particular dislike for? Cartoon characters, figures from movies, that kind of thing?'

'I'm not sure what this has to do with anything—'

'Probably nothing at all,' Slim said. 'I'm just trying to establish whether Emily's behaviour or actions might have been compromised by a particular dislike or a phobia towards something. It's possible such a situation might have made her vulnerable to a certain type of predator.'

Georgia gave a sharp shake of the head as though Slim

were accusing her of something directly. 'Not that I can think of. She was never much into Disney or anything, but she didn't hate it or anything like that. She would just change the channel.'

'Was she into horror movies? Did she obsess over any series of book?'

Georgia shrugged. 'I could ask James when he gets back.'

'That might help. Would you like to talk to Emily about it? That would probably be for the best. She's coming back in a day or two.'

The deadline for their daughter's return had extended again. Slim chose not to comment.

'I'd certainly like to speak to her at some point,' Slim said. 'For the time being I'm still working on background information. One last question and then I'll get out of your hair for the evening. Did she have a mobile phone?'

Georgia tensed. 'She did,' she said slowly. 'She had it when she was taken. The police were able to trace it for the remainder of that first day, but after that, the signal died.'

'And where did they trace it to, if you don't mind me asking?'

Georgia shuddered. Staring at the tabletop, she wiped away a tear.

'Right here,' she said. 'In Emily's room.'

Slim felt a cold sweat break out on his back. 'So, it appears that at some point on that first day, Emily came back?'

Georgia sniffed. 'That's what the police believed,' she said. 'That or someone with her phone did.'

9

James must have returned later than Slim went to bed, because he never heard the man of the house come in. He was there the next morning, though, bouncing around in the hallway, wanting to help as Slim sipped a coffee at the dining room table and Georgia bustled, as full of energy as ever, in the kitchen. He offered to act as Slim's driver, and while Slim saw it as a good opportunity to grill the man for some information, he had a few things to attend to in the town first.

He arranged for James to pick him up at one o'clock, then walked up into Launceston and headed for the local library, where he first searched the local catalogue and then logged on to the internet.

Unsurprisingly, there was no mention anywhere of any such person known as The Woodland Man, but the generic nature of the term made searching for it difficult. Frustrated, instead he searched through all the popular social media sites to see if Emily had an online presence.

Nothing, not so much as a neglected Facebook page. Of course, since the rise in cyber crime and online stalking, many kids now hid behind online alter-egos only shared with their friends. Donald Lane, an expert in digging up details of people's lives, might be able to help, but it would be easier if Slim could get in through a more central door. Or perhaps it really was a buck in the curve and Emily had no online presence. Without her phone, it would be hard to prove.

Next, he turned his attention to Bernadette. It wasn't hard to find the girl's profile, but she had everything set to private, and her profile picture was just a bunch of daffodils in a field. Nothing to give away any clues. Slim considered sending her a friend request, but it was easier to befriend her in the real world first.

Continuing his search, he accessed the secondary school website, and spent some time browsing its various pages, everything from the listed curriculum to the lunch menu. It had a linked blog, but even though Slim scrolled back several years, the content centred around dull posts listing sporting or cultural events. There was only one post of significant interest, dated a week after Emily's return, stating simply, "*In light of recent events, the school requires that all pupils walk to and from school in pairs or groups, avoiding poorly lit areas.*" No mention of what incident might have caused such a request. Suspicious, Slim checked the dates of the surrounding posts and found a potentially important gap of several days during which Emily was missing. There were no requests for help or information, but Slim began to wonder what might have been deleted. Sometimes deleted content was moved to a holding folder rather than being entirely erased. If Slim could crack the website maybe he could find out what the deleted messages had said.

With time to kill, he browsed some local news websites, reading over the official reports concerning Emily's disappearance. It had never quite taken off in the national press, with a few brief articles reciting the facts.

"A Launceston schoolgirl, Emily Martin, 14, disappeared June 12th, 2018. Emily was last seen on the morning of June 12th. Having apparently complained of a headache, friends claimed she had left for home before lunch. Expected to be staying for an after school netball club, Emily's disappearance wasn't discovered until she failed to return home that night. The seven-hour window between her disappearance and the notification of the police is crucial in tracing her whereabouts. If you have any information which might help, please call: —"

An article in the same publication nine days later summed everything up:

"Missing schoolgirl Emily Martin has been found safe and apparently unharmed. On the morning of June 20th, Emily was discovered unconscious in woodland less than three miles from where she was taken. Emily was revived on the way to hospital and is expected to make a full recovery. No suspects have yet been apprehended. Emily is currently aiding police with their enquiries."

And from there it tailed off. With Emily seemingly unable to provide the police with any information, the search for suspects had come to a halt. The case might be officially unsolved, but with no new information, it was effectively closed.

James was waiting in the car, reading a newspaper, when Slim came outside, clearly having been there for some time. Slim climbed in, and James took them across town, heading for Pencott Beach, north of Bude, a small seaside town about thirty minutes away.

'Everything coming along well, I hope,' James said, not quite framing it as a question.

'I'm doing what I can,' Slim said. 'Between you and me, there's not much to go on.' Wondering whether attempting to create a wedge of conspiracy between James and his wife was a masterstroke or a folly likely to end with his termination, he added, 'It would be nice if I could get a word with Emily. Is there something I'm not being told? I mean, Georgia keeps saying that Emily will be back in a couple of days, but I'm yet to see any sign of her.'

James winced, drumming his fingers nervously on the steering wheel. 'Georgia hasn't told you, has she? Nothing surprising about that. She always did want a plant to grow without being watered. This is her thing, so I said I'd keep out of it as much as possible, but between you and me, I wouldn't hold your breath about talking to Emily. Getting hold of her won't be easy.'

Slim sensed his worse fears were coming true. 'No?'

'She, ah, walked out,' James said, grimacing as though tasting something unpleasant. 'The very day of her sixteenth birthday. Georgia had done a cake and everything. Presents, banners on the wall. The lot. Emily walked in, rolled her eyes, and then walked right back out again, out of our lives. You see, Georgia's not only trying to find out what happened two years ago, but she's trying to bring our little girl back in from the cold. And—between you and me—I don't think she can.'

10

THE BEACH AT PENCOTT WAS SHINGLY, PATCHES OF GREY sand appearing like moon pools on its uneven surface. Slim stood on one, hands in his pockets, staring out at the blue-grey rollers battering the shore, while the wind shook stubborn patches of grass on the cliffs behind.

Standing beside him, James shifted from foot to foot, hands buried deep into his pockets, enjoying the wilds of nature far less. For the third or fourth time since they had reached the foreshore from a narrow, winding path, he said, 'The police said that the sand between her toes … it was almost certainly from here. The texture, the geological composition, the varieties of rock.' A shrug. 'Everything.'

Slim glanced up and down the beach. It was remote, not a house to be seen, only a coastguard station on a distant headland, almost hidden in a fogbank slowly closing down the coast from the north.

'Or taken from here,' he said. 'Construction, maybe. A child's sandpit even.'

James gave a short laugh. 'And they'd take the sand from here?'

Eight Days

'They might. It's remote. There are laws about removing sand and stones from beaches these days. They might have come somewhere quiet to do it in secret.'

'And hauled it up that cliff path?'

Slim shrugged. It had been an admittedly long and arduous walk from the clifftop car park, across fields and then down the path. Not an easy hike carrying any sort of load, particularly an unnecessary one.

'What did the police say?'

'That she'd come here, or was brought here. They were never entirely convinced it was an abduction.'

'That's not what Georgia says.'

Again, that wedge. Slim made a mental note to be sure such division had a reason. With the daughter estranged, all her parents had was each other.

'They didn't have enough to go on. She had no marks on her, nothing unusual in her bloodstream. What were they supposed to think? Between you and me, I think they just went through the motions for a while and then let it go.'

Slim turned around, looking up at the cliffs. 'It's the kind of place you could hide a while.'

'There are a couple of chalets up the road a little way,' James said. 'The police searched them, however. They found no signs anyone had been hanging out there.'

Slim nodded. He remembered their conversation in the car.

'And Emily wants this let go? That's why she left?'

James shrugged and sighed, then kicked at a loose stone, sending it tumbling across the rocks to plop into the shore break.

'Georgia is like a hound. She wanted answers, and she was convinced Emily had them. Once the initial shock was over and it was clear Emily's physical health hadn't suffered, she badgered the poor girl constantly as though Emily could turn on her memories like a tap. It didn't go down well. Those years aren't the easiest for a teenage girl in any case, but Georgia wouldn't let it go. And there was something else ... how can I explain it? The girl needed a loving touch, not constant harassment. But my wife ... she acted like the girl had done something wrong and she was going to prove it. In the end, Emily packed her bags. She's staying in Tavistock and going to night classes for her A-levels, so I believe. She's refusing to see us. Georgia is delusional. She thinks the girl is coming home any day.'

Slim nodded. He looked up and down the beach, charting a possible walking route through the rocks.

'Do you mind giving me a few minutes?' he asked. 'I just want to have a look around.'

'Sure.' James looked pleased, released from his shackles. 'I'll wait in the car.'

Slim watched him hike quickly back over the rocks towards the path. Then, picking his own way along the shore, he walked northwards for a few hundred metres until the cliffs converged with the sea and cut him off. Staying just back from the crashing shore break, he stared out at the water, wondering what might cause someone to come down here, then turned his gaze to the cliffs, looking for caves bored into the rock. There were none of significance, the cliff being crumbly here and easily worn away. Looking south, there were no properties to be seen, the rugged coastline forcing habitation inland. The nearest town, Bude, was five miles south, hidden by the cliffs.

He climbed up the foreshore and walked back along the high tide line. Here, where no one came to forage or clean the beach, he found tangles of old fishing net, dented and white-washed buoys torn from lobster pot moorings, lumps of gnarled driftwood, bleached white ovals of cuttlefish bones, a few rusted tin cans, even the remains of a shoe crusted with barnacles.

It made no sense that someone would bring a kidnapped girl down here. It made no sense either that anyone would take shingle from the beach and allow a kidnapped girl to walk in it.

He sighed. A lot of things about this case made no sense.

And it looked like Emily wouldn't be available to answer any questions after all.

But there was a way to get a look at her, one which he could pull off without causing suspicion. Slim bent down, pushing a hand between the rocks until his fingers closed over damp sand. He smiled at the pleasant sensation of rubbing it in his fingers, before scooping a couple of handfuls into his jacket pocket. Then, standing up, he pulled out his phone and held it over his head, wondering if he could pick up a signal here or whether he'd have to wait until he got back to the car.

11

'Slim, it's Don. Is now a good time?'

Slim took a sip from a paper cup of coffee he had bought in the Costa up in Launceston town square, then put it down on the bench beside him and said, 'Sure.'

'I don't know if any of this will help you, but I did manage to find a little dirt on the Martin family.'

'Right. Give me a summary.'

'Mostly to do with James Martin. From 1994 to 1999 he ran a small financial services company. It went out of business. Several employees sued for loss of earnings and pension funds. He filed for bankruptcy and ended up doing a few months for money laundering. His employees got nothing out of it in the end. I actually managed to contact one. I was told at the time that they felt James had used their pension funds to pay a lawyer to get him off more serious charges.'

'Interesting. He doesn't come across as the kind of guy to have done time.'

'He was in with all the financial crooks, not the serial

Eight Days

killers. Easy life. He did, however, get banned from owning any kind of business for ten years. There was also a rumour he had an affair with a colleague. I didn't contact the person in question, but I could get a name and current address if you want it.'

'I do. Just in case. I wonder how Georgia reacted.'

'This was before his current wife,' Don said. 'He married Georgia in 2001. His first wife divorced him shortly after he went down.'

Slim whistled through his teeth. Georgia and James had come across as a life partnership, one that might have struggled for children until both were closing in on middle age. That their history was more recent, that there could be unanticipated footnotes, was a genuine surprise.

'His ex-wife ... is she still alive?'

'No. She died in 2009. Traffic accident. I checked for possible suspicious circumstances, but found none. A lorry overturned in icy conditions. It hit her straight on.'

'I wonder if he knows. That's great, Don. Anything else? What about her?'

'Mrs Martin? Nothing. No prior marriages or scandals I could uncover. She worked as a nursery teacher for a number of years. Her parents both died of complications related to dementia. She nursed them through their last years.'

Slim nodded. That explained Georgia's "bedside manner", as Slim would put it. The homeliness that made him both feel at ease and mothered in a way that his own mother never had. The penchant she had for home cooking when James enjoyed a sly bag of chips. Could there be skeletons in her closet somewhere too?

Leading a quiet life didn't mean she was hiding something. It often meant just that, a life of little consequence, kindly called safe, unkindly considered boring. When he thought of his own misfortune and misadventures, he felt no little envy for an existence of simple family gatherings, afternoon tea served on the patio, and summer evening gardening.

He gave Don a local post office address he had registered with to fax copies of his notes. While it was true that most abductions were committed by someone known to the abducted—usually a family member—even the nicest people took exception to being investigated. He doubted the Martins were any different.

He hung up, then left the castle grounds where he had been sitting with a view over the hill of Polson, and headed back across town. By three o'clock he was sitting on the bench where he had first met Bernadette a few days before. Flipping through a pile of notes, he didn't need to look for her. The crunch of footsteps through the grass gave her away.

'You weren't waiting for me, were you?' she said. 'Because that would be weird.'

'I like the ducks,' Slim said, nodding at the cluster of birds skirting the reefs on the opposite side of the pond. 'Their lives look so easy.'

'Lucky them.'

Bernadette huffed. The temperature was pleasant for this time of year, and her cheeks glowed with the sun's warmth. Slim noticed a couple of spots which had burst on her jaw, becoming red and inflamed. Slim shifted across the seat to give her room to sit down, but she continued standing, watching him.

'So are you really a private investigator, or were you running me a line?'

'I really am, for better or worse. Do you think you could tell me more about what you said the other day? I'd

Eight Days

like to know what you think about the disappearance of Emily Martin.'

'Why do you care what I think? No one else does.'

'I'm not one of your classmates.' Slim held back from telling her what he really thought, that a loner like Bernadette, on top of being naturally suspicious, likely had a lot more thinking time than other kids her age. And her forced isolation from the surrounding society meant word of his questions was unlikely to spread.

Slim shifted across the seat until he was perched on the very end. Eventually, like a shy bird, Bernadette came and sat down, putting her bag between them as though to create a safety barrier.

As she looked up at him, he noticed the remnants of a purplish bruise around her right eye.

'You walked into a door?' he said, nodding at her face.

Bernadette shrugged and looked at her feet. 'Something like that.'

'You gave the door a bit of lip and it swung at you pretty hard? And it stank of booze?'

Bernadette gave a brief smile. 'Huh. I can see why you're a private investigator.'

Slim felt a knot in his stomach tightening, as though someone had reached inside and clenched his intestines in a closed fist. He felt the old rage, the one that usually came with drinking, the one which had left as many scars on his knuckles as it had in the shadows of his face.

'Leave as soon as you can,' he said, wishing he could say something more. 'And don't look back.'

'That's the plan,' Bernadette said, although her voice lacked conviction. Despite her brusque, combative exterior, inside was a girl with a melted heart, her resolve broken from years of abuse. Slim had seen it all before, and it never got easier.

'You asked me what I thought about Emily Martin,' Bernadette said, as though wanting to move the subject on. 'What I think is she was being stalked. Like, some guy was watching her for a while. When he had his chance, he grabbed her.'

'And what did he do with her for eight days?'

'He scared her. That's all. He scared the absolute living crap out of her and she couldn't take it. They said there were no marks on her body at all, but her cheeks were chapped so bad that it looked like she'd cried constantly for days—'

'Where did you read that?'

'The doctor's report.'

'And where did you get that?'

Bernadette shrugged. 'Downloaded it off the net. It's all up there if you know where to look.'

'And where's that?'

'The dark web.'

Slim gave a slow nod. He knew of it, of course, but only by reputation. He had long suspected Donald Lane used it for gathering a lot of his information, but Slim had never had cause to enter it himself. While he was aware many of the urban myths associated with it were likely just that, it was the kind of place he was still keen to avoid. Like the drinking, it had the potential to suck you in and never let you out.

'I'd very much like to see a copy,' Slim said.

Bernadette beamed. 'I could totally get you one,' she said.

'Is there much other information on there?'

Bernadette shrugged. 'Depends what you're after.'

'The Woodland Man.'

Bernadette stared at him for a long time, her eyes

watery as though reliving some childhood panic attack from which she had never quite recovered.

'There might be,' she said.

'Could you look it up for me?'

Bernadette shifted. 'Couldn't you do it for yourself? I try to put that crap out of my mind. I have enough nightmares about it as it is.'

12

Wearing a light blue rain jacket he had picked up in a charity shop, along with a pair of glasses and a generic baseball cap, Slim made his way up the steep road to the Newport estate on which Dave Brockhill lived. With a fake name card around his neck and a clipboard under his arm, he was back in familiar territory under the guise of Mike Lewis, BBC researcher.

He located Dave Brockhill's place, then did a couple of circuits of the estate, getting a look at the house from as many angles as he could. It was generic, semi-detached, two up, two down, with a garage on its outer side, a short driveway on which a blue Mazda was parked. The garden was neat at the front, hidden by a wooden fence at the back.

Trying to ask the man straight out for the information he wanted would never work, so Slim needed a cover and had to hope the man was a talker. To get into the mood, he picked a couple of houses at random, knocked on the doors, and spent a few minutes asking each person who answered a few vague questions about local history. By the

Eight Days

time he walked up the sloping drive to Brockhill's front door, he almost believed who he said he was.

Brockhill answered on the second knock. Wearing painting overalls and with a pencil tucked behind one lopsided ear, he looked like an archetypal DIY enthusiast, brushing off dust and then leaning on the door frame with one leg crossed in front of the other.

'Yeah? What are you after? I'm not buying anything so don't even go there.'

Slim introduced himself as Mike Lewis and explained he was doing preliminary research for a potential documentary on the area's history. He told Brockhill he had been door-knocking in the hope of finding interesting people worth inviting to a televised interview.

At the suggestion, Brockhill gave a firm shake of the head. 'Mate, I'll tell you some anecdotes or whatever, but I don't want my face on a TV screen.'

'That's fair enough. But you're willing to answer a few questions.'

Slim framed it as a statement rather than a question, and the subliminal intention worked. Brockhill shrugged and nodded. 'Sure.'

He led Slim into a brightly lit place thick with the scent of fresh paint. The signs of redecoration were everywhere, with a stepladder in the hallway beside a stack of emulsion paint tins and a pile of old sheets. Masking tape covered skirting boards and through one open door Slim saw sheets covering living room furniture.

'I'm sorry if I'm interrupting,' Slim said, as Brockhill led him through into a small kitchen which was an oasis of normal amongst the upheaval of the rest of the house.

Brockhill shrugged. 'You're not. I'm retired and divorced, so I have all the time in the world.' He spread paint-stained fingers and cackled a garrulous laugh which made Slim feel uncomfortable. 'Brew? You a tea or coffee man?'

In the guise of Mike Lewis, Slim tried to hide his regret as he said, 'Tea.'

Brockhill chatted amiably as he made their drinks, making himself a cup of instant from a decent brand Slim approved of, then passing Slim a cup of tea so weak he could have left a cup sat in the rain and collected more flavour. Trying not to wince as he took a sip, Slim said, 'You make a decent cup. Been on your own long? My own wife ditched me for a supposed mate. Shouldn't be talking like that though.' He chuckled. 'Not very professional of me, is it?'

Brockhill laughed. 'Did you put his head through a wall?'

'Would've done if I could've caught him. They went overseas.'

'Cowards. No one else involved with mine. No one would have wanted her. Upped sticks after I had a bit of trouble at work.'

Slim sensed Brockhill wanted to talk, so he purposely deflected the attempt, aware Brockhill would come back around to it when he was ready.

'Woman was a fool with a man like you. Decorating looks like it's going well.' He pointed at a wooden arch leading through into a small dining room. 'You do that yourself?'

'Sure did. Wife never appreciated it. Took down a wall mirror when I knocked it through. I had to look at her; no reason why she had to look at herself.'

Brockhill cackled again, and Slim wondered how much was true and how much was bitter humour. He was still thinking how to respond when Brockhill continued, 'So, local history, is it? Can't tell you much except what I might have heard before I got barred from the pub.'

Again, Slim didn't press for information. Brockhill was like a book left open with its pages flapping in the wind, calling to be read. In truth, Slim could guess why Brockhill had been barred and why his wife had left him. It was the underlying cause and Brockhill's opinion on that which he wanted to unearth.

'Do you go up to the castle much?' Slim asked.

Brockhill shrugged. 'Walked through the grounds from time to time. Bit of a sod of a hill so these days I usually drive.'

Slim, who had walked through the steep valley between Launceston and Newport on the way but planned to take a bus back, nodded. 'I can understand,' he said. 'Quite the place, though. I imagine there's a few legends connected with it for sure.'

Brockhill shrugged. 'Shop sells guides,' he said. 'That all you're after?'

Slim shook his head. 'That's no good to me. Like you say, all that's in books or online. I need something deeper. Stuff that's never been written down. Secret stuff, the kind of thing people don't like to talk about.'

'I imagine there's a lot of that. Not sure if I'd know any of it. Before I got ostracised from society all I did much was work and watch TV. Pub on Friday nights, but all we talked about until the shit went down was the next afternoon's games. What team are you?'

Slim smiled, remembering an old acquaintance. 'QPR,' he said. 'For better or worse.'

'Christ. Painful days, I imagine.'

Slim was keen to ask what had got Brockhill ostracised from society, but knew the man was willing to tell, so again skirted around asking a direct question. Instead, he pulled out a legend he had made up on the walk over about an old woman who supposedly haunted the castle grounds.

Brockhill listened to the story with a frown, then started to laugh. 'Pretty sure someone was pulling your leg with that. Never heard of no Old Joan. And certainly no missing kids back in the fifties. Be well known, that would.'

'And what about the Woodland Man?' Slim asked, pulling his trump card. 'I heard something about a man haunting local forests—'

Brockhill banged a hand down on the table. 'Stop right there. Where are you getting this kind of crap?'

'I heard it—'

'Well you heard it wrong. That's not a myth, it's a made-up kids' story.'

'I heard the name mentioned in connection with a disappearance—'

'And reappearance, don't forget. Is that what this is about? That girl? You know I was a suspect, don't you? Are you from the tabloids? She showed up, don't forget. If I'd had anything to do with it, the police would know by now. That damn case cost me my marriage and my job. I got barred from my local, but not before a group of guys I thought were my friends took me round the back and beat seven bells out of me. And all over nothing. I got released without charge.' Brockhill hit the tabletop again, but with less conviction this time. 'I lost everything, all because of a stupid fairy story.'

Slim waited until Brockhill had finished, then counted to fifteen under his breath, giving the man time to calm down but leaving space in case he had anything else to say.

'You know,' Brockhill said, again taking the bait, as though silence was not something he could endure, 'that was all made up, don't you? Mrs Cleave, up at the primary school. That old witch. She made it up to scare the kids

Eight Days

into line. She started up with it back in my day, when I was just a nipper.'

'I've never heard of her.'

Brockhill shrugged. 'She'd be ninety if a day younger by now,' he said. 'Retired, not before time. That woman hated children. People said she got into teaching to take her revenge on the young of the world. But, damn if kids leaving her class didn't have respect. Some say this town's only gone downhill now she's not conditioning the kids.'

'And she made up this story about the so-called Woodland Man?'

Brockhill gave a little chuckle. 'No doubt the details have changed over the years, but in my day there was a stand of trees out behind the primary school. It's gone now, replaced by a builder's merchant. She'd sit us down for story time in the afternoon, point out the trees and tell us she could see him back there, watching. Always watching. We'd jerk our heads around, peer out of the window, but of course there'd be no one there.'

'Just a story.'

'Ha, well, wait for it.' Brockhill shifted uncomfortably on his chair, then scratched at the back of his head. 'She'd always tell the same kind of story. He had once been a regular guy, like you or me. He had a kid in the school, and he told them always to wait, never ever to leave school until he arrived. One day, he had been on his way to pick up his kid from school, when he'd been in a car accident and ended up all burned. His kid—usually a she but sometimes he, depending on the way Mrs Cleave told it that day, sometimes even a couple of kids—got tired of waiting and decided to walk home.

'The kid disappeared into thin air. And the guy, when he finally came out of hospital all disfigured and the like, would show up to keep watch on the school, still waiting for his kid. And if you were unlucky, and he mistakenly thought you were his—because his eyesight had been damaged, you see—he would think it was you and follow you home.'

'Why would he mistake you?'

'See, that was how she got us into line. This guy would recognise you not on looks but on behaviour. His kid was real boisterous, misbehaving, back-talking the teacher. Anyone doing the same would be a prime target, and it was said you didn't want him after you. He wasn't a nice guy, you see.'

'Why not?'

'He would take you off somewhere and punish you for misbehaving. And if you ever came back, you might look like the same kid on the outside, but inside, behind your eyes, someone else would be looking out. Because once you'd been taken by the Woodland Man, you could never be the same ever again.'

13

Brockhill shivered. 'Christ, I need a drink after that.' He went to a cupboard and pulled out a bottle of cheap whisky. Taking a tumbler from another cupboard, he turned to Slim and said, 'You drink? Want one?'

Slim stared at the whisky, feeling all the old desires come rushing back into the room like unwelcome friends. 'No,' he forced himself to say. 'Not on duty.'

Brockhill shrugged. 'Ah well. You mind if I do?'

Slim did, because it left him unable to concentrate, but he shook his head. 'Go ahead,' he said.

'I'll make you another brew,' Brockhill said, reaching for the kettle, the tumbler in his free hand. Slim stared at it like a hypnotist's watch, aware he needed to leave as soon as possible. Attempting to change the subject, he said, 'So this story was entirely made up? You never saw the so-called Woodland Man?'

'Only once,' Brockhill said. 'On the very last day of term. Walking out of school for the very last time, I heard a scream go up from one of the girls, then saw someone pointing. Back there in the trees a man was standing, motionless, just watching us. We all knew it was him so we ran like there was fire in our pants. The last thing of that school I ever saw when I glanced back was old Mrs Cleave, standing by her classroom window, arms folded, watching us, a smile on her ugly old face. Then I ran like hell. I was so scared I pissed my pants. Eleven years old and I pissed myself. Father gave me the cane for that.'

Brockhill smiled as though the years had softened the memory of corporal punishment into something kinder, wistful. Slim said, 'How could you be sure it was him?'

'Because he looked just right, exactly as she'd told us so many times. He even had the bird perched on his finger.'

'A bird?'

'Yeah, one of his pets. Well, the way she told it, he'd lost everything after his accident. His kid had disappeared, and his wife and family had disowned him. Society shunned him, so he took up living in the woods, hence his name. And his only friend was a little yellow bird, a canary, which had escaped from somewhere or other. Mrs Cleave always told us that if you heard the sound of a canary tweeting, you should never, ever turn around, because it would be him, standing behind you. It put the fear of God into us. Canaries became such an unpopular pet around town that to this day you can go down to the pet shop on Newport Industrial Estate and there's no bird section. The nearest place you can get them is way out of town.'

Brockhill sipped the whisky and put the glass down on the table. It was all Slim could do not to swipe it away and finish the contents.

'You thought it was him?' he croaked. 'The figure in the woods?'

Brockhill shook his head. 'I know now that the sadistic old cow probably set us up. Most likely it was the school caretaker or one of the other teachers back there dressed

Eight Days

up to look like him. Her way of saying goodbye. But I never, ever set foot in those woods, and to this day I'm not a fan of anywhere with trees. It's like he's always there, watching. The irony is that I got accused of being him when that girl disappeared.'

Slim had found the story fascinating, but Brockhill was finally coming around to the part he really wanted. He only hoped the man would keep it short. He watched Brockhill pour another drink and wondered how long he could resist. He had dried out in prison but realised now that once a drinker, he would always be one. It would be so easy to join the man, finish the bottle and then stumble off into the afternoon, find somewhere close by where he could procure more, then slowly give himself over to oblivion. His drinker's mind was already working overtime, recalling every pub, corner shop and off-license he had passed on the way, counting how much money he had in his wallet, calculating what would be the best purchase, and where would be the safest place to go and wreck himself. Where he would sleep, where he would throw up, where he would wander to avoid trouble, the pubs that looked most respectable, where he was least likely to get beaten up when the drink inevitably led him to run his mouth. And as the dark thoughts encircled his mind like a flock of angry birds, on the inside he felt only a deep, bitter sadness, a knowledge that the beast he thought he had finally defeated was still there waiting in the darkness, and longing to be free.

He almost didn't hear as Brockhill said, 'You know what kids are like. In truth, Mrs Cleave probably only told us that story a couple of times, but our imaginations ran with it. Kids would tell other kids newer, more violent versions; bullies would use it as a tool. I remember there was this girl who got picked on. I was in the fourth or fifth year at secondary school. Quiet girl, didn't know her much. Someone put a dead canary in her locker.'

Brockhill picked up the glass and drained it, then immediately poured another. 'I was in the locker room at the time,' he continued. 'Quiet girl, I said, but I never heard a shriek like it. Turned my blood. People were trying to calm her down, others were laughing. Never did find out who put it in there, but she didn't show up at school the next day, or the day after that. A few days later it was announced in a special assembly that she had died. They didn't tell us how, but of course it wasn't long before the truth got out. Turned out she went into the woods and hung herself from a tree.'

'Good God.'

Brockhill shrugged. 'The power of that bloody story. And this was years after we'd left primary school. It still had a hold on us.'

Slim glanced down at his clipboard. He had written nothing. He quickly jotted down Mrs Cleave's name and a couple of other details, then asked Brockhill if he remembered the dead girl's name.

'Not sure now,' he said. 'I think her first name was Susan. We called her Smelly Sue.'

Slim didn't comment on the cruelty of the name. He had been a kid once, too. He jotted down the name and looked up, dismayed to see Brockhill pulling a second glass out of the cupboard.

'You might as well,' he said, grinning. 'I've seen you eyeing up the bottle. Don't worry, the pigs are half asleep around here. Just don't run into the back of anyone.'

Slim realised he was referring to a car and assumed Slim was driving. Slim saw one last chance to escape before it was too late and stood up quickly, nearly knocking over his chair.

'I really need to push on,' he said. 'I have other calls to make. But thank you kindly for your time.'

Brockhill gave the glass a forlorn look and then shrugged. 'A pleasure. If you want to continue our chat, stop by whenever you want. I'm not exactly overloaded with guests.'

'I appreciate it,' Slim said, then he was triumphantly, mercifully heading for the front door, his eyes glazed, his hands shaking so violently with booze lust that he held the clipboard to his chest as tightly as a precious child. He didn't know what, if anything, Brockhill said as he let Slim outside, but then the door was closing and he could breathe once again. He was breathing in beautiful fresh air, and he could look up and let his vision clear and see that a man was standing beside a tree and watching him, hands in pockets, from the other side of the street.

14

'What are you doing up here?' James said, frowning as he crossed the street. 'Isn't that Dave Brockhill's place?'

Slim, who wanted to ask James the same question, just nodded. 'Following up a lead,' he said.

'Chap got released without charge,' James said, as though that put an end to it. 'Car's parked up round the corner. You want a lift back across town?'

Slim hadn't even considered how he would make it past the temptation of the town's pubs and off-licenses, but now he saw a lifeline. 'If you could drop me at the library, that would be great,' he said.

'Sure thing. Follow me.'

Slim didn't get a chance to ask why James was wandering around the nondescript housing estate until they got back to the car.

'Popped in to see a friend,' James said, clearing up the matter. 'Was on the way back from Homeleigh.'

Slim had seen the signs to the large out-of-town garden centre just past the estate. While that might clear up part of the matter, it didn't explain why James had ignored a

Eight Days

dozen or more clear parking spaces in order to park some distance away from where Slim had seen him, nor why he was wearing his jacket with the hood up when it was neither raining nor particularly cold. Questions for another day.

'Georgia keeps asking me how you're getting on,' James said, as they pulled out onto the main road. 'I think she sees me as your assistant or something,' he added with a matey smile which made Slim uncomfortable.

'I'm getting there,' he said. 'I'm still reviewing the case background, looking for clues the police might have missed.'

'Anything interesting?'

Slim shrugged. He sensed a hint of frustration behind James's questions. While Georgia might still be gung-ho for the investigation, James was probably frustrated about sharing his house with a near stranger, and aware that the costs of Slim's day rate were racking up on what he had made no secret of believing was a wasted operation.

'I'm hoping to have more to go on soon.' Then, twisting the knife, he added, 'It would be helpful if your wife was honest about Emily.'

'She'd have to be honest with herself first,' James said. 'She's convinced the girl will be home any day.' He shook his head. 'Won't happen. We don't even get a phone call.'

Slim let the conversation die as they headed across town. When James stopped outside the library he asked only when Slim would be back for dinner.

Remembering what he had scheduled, Slim shook his head. 'I'll be back late tonight,' he said. 'I'm following up a lead. I'll just grab a bag of chips on the way back.'

James looked briefly envious before wishing Slim good luck and pulling off. Slim watched the car until it turned out of sight, wondering what the man might be hiding.

On the computer he found an obituary for Norma Cleave of Polson, Launceston. She had died in 2012 at the age of 92, which by Slim's estimation would have put her within a few years of retirement even in Dave Brockhill's schooldays. There was no way Emily or Bernadette could have heard the story from its original source, which meant either a teacher was retelling it or the kids themselves were passing the story on. Primary school kids had the most active of imaginations, so no doubt the story had evolved and mutated over the years. On a whim he decided to check out the local primary school's website, and there, to his surprise, he found it.

It came up in recurring blogs around summer time. By the look of things, the Woodland Man had been adapted as a quasi-summer solstice figure and champion for the environment. A blog from three years ago had pictures of a pupils' wall display, a couple of dozen children's depictions in paint and crayon of a stumbling figure with trees for legs and birds perched on his shoulders. *Welcome the Woodland Man to our school*, read a banner across the top, and in some pictures the children had drawn depictions of themselves waving or beckoning.

Slim checked the details, then looked back at previous yearly blogs. The Year Four pupils each time. He looked for the name of the teacher: Mrs May. In one class photo he found her, youthful, smiling, her arms folded, a confident look on her face.

It wouldn't be hard to track her down. In fact, she probably still worked at the school. Slim made a note, then cycled back through a few years of blogs and downloaded all the pictures of the pupils' displays that he could find. Then, using a separate photograph program, he zoomed in and attempted to read the pupil's names written along the bottom of each display. A few were barely legible, but in each case he was able to identify enough letters to confirm the name was not the one he was looking for: Emily Martin. He knew she had gone to this primary school from what Georgia had said, and even though he was fairly certain what year she would have passed through the Fourth Year, he checked a couple of years either side, on the unlikely chance she had been held back or pushed forward.

But ... nothing. For whatever reason, Emily Martin had offered no contribution to the Woodland Man wall display.

And Slim needed to know why.

15

He felt a sense of nostalgia alighting from the bus to his first visit to the pretty Devonshire town of Tavistock for a couple of years, but he didn't have much time to appreciate the quaint historic streets nestled in the river valley on the edge of Dartmoor because the bus's arrival had left him barely enough time to get to the community college before the start of his class. In fact, by the time he arrived and had signed in, he was several minutes late. A staff member led him to the correct room, where the teacher paused the class long enough for Slim to introduce himself and give a bumbling account of why he had chosen to take a night class in A-level mathematics. Taking a seat near the back as the class resumed, he was able to take stock of the other students, a mixture of scruffy school dropouts and older people wanting a second chance. Firmly in the latter category, Slim made a show of making notes while establishing which of the other students was Emily Martin.

From behind it was initially difficult to tell, but as a girl in the front corner looked across the room while poking herself in the cheek with a pencil, Slim recognised a profile view of a girl he had seen staring at him from the Martins' mantelpiece.

It appeared that she was an eager student. While briefly unsettled by the entrance of a newcomer, a couple of other kids got back to talking about anything other than the subject material while the teacher droned on at the front, seemingly oblivious. Emily had her head down, scribbling away with a frenetic energy Slim found surprising. Even had he written down every equation and word the teacher said, Slim would have had his pen in the air most of the time. He watched the way her shoulders moved with the action in an exaggerated manner, wondering if she suffered from some form of autism.

The class cut for a fifteen-minute break, and Slim followed the others down the corridor to a common room with a couple of drinks machines. Emily pulled a flask from her bag and sat down on a sofa chair near a window. Slim bought a cup of coffee from a machine and found a position near the wall from where he could surreptitiously watch her.

She wore jeans and a no-brand sweater she had likely bought in a supermarket's clothing section. Her lack of fashion awareness was itself a cause for concern in a girl of sixteen, but more unsettling was that she seemed unable to look away from the window. She held her books over her knees, but every few seconds she would lift her head and peer out through the glass, as though waiting for someone or something to appear outside.

Slim couldn't approach her without causing suspicion, so he contented himself with observing her for a few minutes before a bell rang and they all headed back for the second hour of the class.

In the classroom again, he resumed his previous

position, continuing his observance of the girl. The teacher began where he had left off, and Emily immediately recommenced her frenetic scribbling. Even though the curtains were drawn, Slim noticed how Emily had chosen to sit as far from the window as possible, and nearest to the door. There were several spare seats around her, and no one else was in such close proximity to the front of the class. Slim wished he could see what she was writing, but if he did something to disturb or upset her, he would lose any chance of eventually engaging her in conversation.

The class ended at nine-thirty. Most of the students filed out, but Emily took her time putting her things away. Slim made a show of reading over a handout he had been given, until the girl finally headed for the door. Still peering at the handout, Slim followed, leaving a safe distance between them as Emily headed for the lobby. There, instead of going straight out through the doors, she waited inside, leaning against a wall with her bag over her shoulder, staring out into the night. Slim, wasting time by adjusting his bag, eventually ran out of things to keep himself busy, so he muttered goodnight, pushed out through the doors, and headed a short distance up the street. Aware he was close to missing the last bus back to Launceston, he sat on a bench then pulled out his phone, pretending to be on a call while keeping one eye on the community centre's entrance.

He couldn't wait for long unless he wanted a cold night of wandering around an empty town. He was just grimacing at his watch when a car pulled in. Emily came running out of the community centre and climbed into the passenger seat. They sped off, passing by where Slim sat.

He frowned. Emily had been sitting in the front, staring straight ahead, when he might have expected to see her conversing over the contents of the class or some other

Eight Days

prolonged greeting. She was quiet, he had established. Fair enough.

Who, though, was the woman driving the car? Neither James nor Georgia was exactly young, so he couldn't expect a grandparent to look in their early forties. Offering no hint of a smile, the woman had faced straight ahead as she drove, as immobile as the girl beside her.

Slim could have brushed it all off or explained it away, except for one thing. While the streetlights and the headlight glare had allowed him only a brief glimpse as the car sped past, he could have been certain the older woman was a spitting image of Emily. So alike they had been in everything from looks and hair to posture and poise, that Slim could have mistaken them as mother and daughter.

16

Georgia was still stalling. Nearly ten days he had stayed with the Martins and she was still pulling the line that Emily would be home soon.

'She's had a hard time of late,' was her latest excuse. 'We don't want to pressure her.'

Slim had said nothing of course about joining the girl's night school class. He had joined another too, A-level geography, tomorrow, having had Don pirate the class lists from the community centre's computer. While getting a delayed education probably wouldn't hurt, he hoped to eventually get a chance to speak to the girl, and also to observe her mysterious companion.

James, as always, was a better source of information. As they drove across town to meet with an old family friend who worked for the local police, Slim asked, 'Just out of interest, does your wife have a sister?'

James's head snapped around. 'What? No, she's an only child. We both were. We always had a really tight family until these troubles started.'

Eight Days

Something in his words caught Slim's attention, but he let it pass.

'You mean Emily's abduction?'

James nodded quickly. Too quickly, Slim thought, although he was reluctant to read anything into it. James always looked nervous when Slim questioned him outside Georgia's presence, as though his mouth was a runaway train he could not control. Slim liked the man's honesty, if he knew to ask the right questions.

'We were doing all right before that happened,' he said. 'Threw a right spanner in the works. If only we knew the truth, who took her....'

'Do you think Emily knows?' Slim asked, carefully watching James's reaction, but the older man just shrugged.

'Maybe deep down,' he said. 'I think it might be one of those traumatic memory loss things, the ones soldiers get.'

'PTSD?'

'That's the one. You know, they used to call it shellshock.'

Slim smiled at the innocence in James's words. This was a man who'd done his worst fighting in a courtroom.

'I served in the first Gulf War,' he said, offering a frailty in the hope James might offer one of his own. 'I was a kid, eighteen, nineteen. It was my only active tour. I know several people who suffered PTSD. Its effects vary. Some black everything out, others are forever haunted.'

James was quiet for a moment, staring straight ahead. Then he said, 'Did you ever watch a man die?'

Again, that strange choice of words. Not *see*, but *watch*, as though you stood by, dumbly fascinated as events uncurled.

It had been a while since Slim had thought about the boots in the sand, still filled with human feet, the rest of the person they had once belonged to reduced to scattered pieces of meat and bone. He closed his eyes.

'Yes,' he said.

~

'Graham is an old family friend,' James said, as they pulled into the driveway of a pretty cottage in a tiny hamlet a few miles outside Launceston. 'He's still active in the Devon & Cornwall Police, but he's agreed to let you see the police file as a personal favour.'

'That's good of him,' Slim said, wondering what the return favour might be.

They walked between colourful flowerbeds to a front door shaded below a porch. It opened before James could knock and a greying, balding man still thick with muscle appeared in the doorway. He wore jeans and a faded t-shirt with a surfing brand logo.

'James, good to see you. And this must be John Hardy. Graham Reeves. Detective, but there's no need for formalities.' He reached out and shook Slim's hand with a powerful grip that stopped just short of being confrontational. 'Normally I'd dismiss a PI as a money-grabbing sham, but I've read about a couple of your cases. Rather unfortunate, that last one.'

Slim resisted the urge to punch the man in the face. No doubt Reeves was as competitive in his job as he might once have been among the Atlantic waves or on a rugby field. As a detective he would have noticed the scuffs on Slim's jacket and recognised a man struggling from month to month, regardless of a few accolades. The BMW in the drive and a jacket hanging up in the hall that likely cost more than Slim's last car proved that a generous pay and benefits package had more value than a little short-lived fame, even if the mockery in Reeves's words masked the envy in his eyes.

'You win some, and you lose some,' Slim said. 'And you tend to fall harder when you lose.'

'Isn't that the truth.'

Reeves led them inside and took them into a wide dining-living room with huge bay windows and a panoramic view of hills rolling away towards Launceston. The room was so bright Slim felt an urge to draw the curtains, but Reeves leaned on a chair and sighed.

'You don't get bored of it,' he said with a pompous smirk. 'And it helps, after a long day in the field. Clears your mind before you head back out to the front. Coffee? Then we'll get down to business.'

Slim found the war reference distasteful, and it did nothing for his growing dislike for the detective, but he focused on the question in hand.

'Black,' he said. 'Brewed yesterday, if possible.'

⸻

Reeves brought out a file and opened it on the table. James, sitting at the end of the table, appeared nervous, as though afraid of what might emerge. Slim, having struggled to get much from the Martins other than speculation, was looking forward to some cold, hard facts.

'You understand that this is still an active case?' Reeves said, looking pointedly at Slim. 'I've had to log this meeting as part of the investigation, to keep it above board, and I can't allow you to take any material away nor make copies.'

'Sure. Are you recording this too?' Slim smiled and nodded at the sideboard. 'That bunch of dried flowers up there. That's where I'd position a camera. In the wicker basket, not among the flowers themselves. Just to ensure stability.'

For the first time Reeves was caught off guard. 'No, I'm not,' he said. 'Would you like me to?'

Slim smiled. 'I'll leave that up to you, Detective.'

Reeves gave Slim a cold smile that clearly indicated their dislike was mutual. Slim preferred it that way. You didn't need to pretend to be friends with someone in order to work with them. In fact, it was often better to establish the parameters of your relationship early on, to avoid any slips farther down the road.

'I might take a walk,' said James, who had remained loitering by the front door as though looking for a chance to get away. Neither Slim nor Reeves disagreed. Through the bay windows Slim watched James walk down the driveway. As soon as the man turned out of sight, Slim said, 'Was he involved?'

Reeves shook his head. 'We found nothing. He's a friend but I'm gathering you know by now a little about his background. You wouldn't be a PI if you didn't specialise in digging up dirt.'

'I make it a priority,' Slim said. 'I know he went to prison. Fraud. But people make mistakes. I just got out. Can't see how it would have any bearing on this case. There really is little to be gained by abducting your own daughter.'

'Nevertheless, suspicion fell on him right the way through,' Reeves said. 'He has a naturally nervous disposition. He looks guilty, and he says things that make him look guilty, even when he's not.'

'I did some time as an interrogator in the army,' Slim said. 'I know the type. He wants to help, almost wants to make you happy with what he says, as though pleasing people is more important than the truth. It can often come

Eight Days

from neglect experienced in childhood. He's looking for praise because he had none growing up.'

'You know your psychology. I'm almost impressed.'

'I was that child,' Slim said. 'Instead of spending my life looking for acceptance, I joined the military and became an alcoholic.'

'We each have a path,' Reeves said. 'Some harder than others.' He rubbed his hands together, as though to put the conversation to bed. 'Right. Where would you like to start?'

'In the middle,' Slim said. 'With Emily's interview. I want to know why the girl wouldn't talk.'

Reeves laughed, and Slim felt his cheeks burn with the anticipation of some clumsily missed oversight. 'My God, you call yourself a private investigator? How long have you been taking the Martins' money? That's the easiest one of all. Because she can't.'

17

'Emily Martin has been nearly mute since birth,' Reeves said, still shaking his head with disbelief. 'She had an infection of her vocal chords as a baby and as a result her ability to speak was inhibited. She can make sounds, but she communicates with sign language. I can't believe they never told you. After she was found we attempted to interview her with a sign language expert, and we also asked her to write down what happened. In both cases she refused to respond. If that girl knows what happened to her during those eight days, we have no way of knowing. The Martins didn't tell you about her disability? That beggars belief. But then, between you and me, they have always been in denial.'

'Besides the speech issue, does Emily suffer any other cognitive ailment?' Slim said, trying to recover from some of the embarrassment he felt. He had glossed over the Martins' reluctance to offer him clear information, but in the presence of this brash, abrasive man, what he had thought was a gentle unfolding of the facts had been reinterpreted as a failure to do his duty.

Eight Days

'You mean, is she retarded?' Reeves said with astonishing insensitivity. Before Slim could even react, he added, 'No, she's not. Went to school like everyone else, did her homework, went to sports club and came home on time. By all accounts, leaving school early on that day was a once-off, not done before or since.'

'Was Emily given any kind of treatment to encourage her to remember?' Slim asked.

Reeves laughed, and Slim found himself clenching his fists beneath the table. He wondered whether the ten years in age and the remnants of his military guile would be enough to overcome a man still undertaking active police training.

'I know you're digging for police incompetence, Slim, but there was none on my watch. Not every corner of every street has a camera, and sometimes people literally do just disappear. Do you know how many unsolved missing persons cases happen every year?'

'I believe it's around fifteen hundred,' Slim said, pleased to knock the smirk off Reeves's face, albeit momentarily.

'At least you've done some homework. To answer your question, we had specialists in the interview room. The girl had ample opportunity to provide information, but she refused. Later, she blamed amnesia, but during the initial interview she refused to answer any questions.'

'Was her mother present?'

Reeves nodded. 'Emily was a minor at the time, so it was required.'

'Okay, so there was no confession. What was the physical evidence?'

'She was in good health. No signs of physical or sexual assault. She allowed a team of doctors to check her. All correct protocol was followed.' Reeves shook his head, for the first time appearing almost human. 'It was as though she could have been living at home the whole time.'

'I heard there was sand between her toes.'

'Yes. As though she'd been walking on a beach. We did a composition analysis comparing it with sand from more than thirty local beaches accessible to the public. The composition of rock types present most closely matched Pencott, five miles north of Bude. We searched all abandoned properties in the area and did some door-knocking, but came up with nothing.' Reeves shrugged. 'Resources are thin. Emily reappeared. What else can I say? Our only witness wouldn't or couldn't provide any information. There have been no other abductions in the area since, so we had to divert our resources elsewhere.'

Slim nodded. From a technical standpoint, he agreed, no matter how emotionally charged Georgia might be. Her daughter was back, unharmed. How easy to forget about those missing eight days?

Frustrated, Slim stood up and walked away from the table, over to the wide bay windows with their panoramic view over the surrounding countryside. Rolling hills stretched away into the hazy distance. A couple of church spires poked out of wooded valleys, and in the far distance Launceston Castle was just visible between two closer hills.

'I like your views,' Slim said. 'In general I'm not a fan of windows. It's too easy for people to see inside.'

'You think someone might have been watching Emily Martin?'

Slim nodded. 'It seems likely, doesn't it? Her window is at the back of the house, overlooking their garden. Someone could easily have watched from the field back there.'

'We considered it. We did background checks on all members of her extended family who live in the area, and

Eight Days

also interviewed a number of dog walkers who frequented the road from where you can access the field behind the Martin property. We had a few leads, but nothing came to anything.'

In the garden outside the window, a tall hedgerow lined with trees hid the road, and a sloping grass lawn in need of a cut extended right up to it. On a terraced section about halfway down, Reeves was in the process of building a patio. An area of sand had been half covered with paving stones. A couple of dozen more leaned against some sandbags from a local builder's merchant.

'What kind of leads?' Slim said.

'The best concerned a young man called Julian Carter. He had been seen by several different people climbing over a gate and running across the field behind the Martins' property. He was recognised by a person who runs a local bakery where Carter is a frequent customer. We pulled him in, named him as a suspect and put the fear of God into him. It turned out he'd been banging the wife of a local doctor. Their property is at the bottom of the field. Carter was sneaking in over the back hedge so he wouldn't be seen going up their drive.' Reeves gave a little laugh and shook his head. 'Honestly, the things people will do for a bit of action. It blows my mind sometimes.'

Slim turned away from the window. Through an archway that led into a kitchen he saw a silver cage sitting on a table, a little golden bird sat inside. Time stood still as he stared at the canary as it shifted sideways along its perch, moving in awkward jerks as though it had something wrong with its feet.

He glanced back at Graham Reeves, standing by the table, arms folded as he leaned over a local gazette left lying open on the tabletop. Whether Reeves had seen Slim notice the bird, Slim didn't know. Slim remembered the description of Reeves that James had given him on the way over.

An old family friend.

And he remembered the description of the Woodland Man from Dave Brockhill.

'His name's Alfred,' Reeves said suddenly, making Slim start. A shrug as he turned around and looked up. 'It was my grandfather's name. He doesn't sing anymore, not since I put him in the cage.'

Cold fingers of dread were creeping along Slim's spine. 'A rare pet in these parts, so I've heard,' he said, throat dry.

Reeves nodded. 'Would you believe where I found him? On the day we discovered Emily Martin in the woods in Polson. He was there, in a tree overlooking the clearing where she was found. Some monster had taped his feet to the branch.'

18

Slim climbed over the gate and into the field. He paused, glancing back up and down the road, wondering if he might've been seen. The foliage was thick and untended around the hedgerow and the road had a slight left-leaning curve; someone would need to be within a few steps to see him climb over.

He glanced at his watch. Then, setting himself, he waited until the second hand reached the top and then started into a run. Fifteen seconds in, and still only halfway to the lower hedge which bordered the doctor's garden, he pulled up, wheezing. Glancing back, however, he saw he was already out of sight of the gate. Setting himself again, he started in a slow walk back up the field.

One minute and nine seconds. Slim frowned. One minute and twenty-four seconds was a narrow window in which to be seen on multiple occasions. He looked across the field in the direction of the Martins' house. The area of hedge at the garden's rear was clearly visible from the gate.

Slim shook his head. The likelihood that this Julian

Carter person had been spotted on recurring occasions running across the field seemed unlikely. Standing at the bottom of the Martins' garden, however, made sense. Slim pulled out his phone.

'Don, it's me.'

'Slim. What can I do for you? How's the case going?'

'Slowly. Listen, I need to establish whether or not there is a connection between a detective of the Cornwall and Devon police and a suspect in the Emily Martin case, called Julian Carter.'

'I'm on it,' Don said. 'I'll call you back in a couple of days.'

Slim hung up. He pulled a flask from the rucksack strapped to his back and took a sip of thick, bitter coffee. A good thing he'd left the military when he did. By now he'd be an embarrassment. The sun was just disappearing behind a bank of threatening rain clouds, so Slim took advantage of the reduced visibility to take a walk around the field's perimeter, aware that from the shadows under the trees bordering the far side of the field he was unlikely to be seen from the houses that backed onto the Launceston side. In truth, only the Martins had a low enough rear hedge that their upper windows could be clearly seen from where the field gave way to a patch of woodland, and the distance was such that only bright colours would be clearly visible from Emily's window, except perhaps shortly before sunset, when the full light of the sun would be directed under the trees. While Slim had entertained the possibility that Emily might have seen someone watching her, she would have needed hawk-like eyes to see anything clearly beyond the midway point of the field.

Giving up for now, he headed back to the house, where he found Georgia furiously polishing horse brasses in the kitchen, the smell of Brasso hanging thickly in the air.

'Does the name Julian Carter ring a bell?' he said by way of greeting.

Georgia immediately tensed. 'A local ruffian,' she said, not looking up. 'Used to come around asking to wash the windows. James shooed him off the property on one occasion, and a few days later the hubcaps went missing from the car.'

'I heard he was a suspect in the case of Emily's abduction.'

'Did Graham tell you? I remember when they pulled him in. I didn't think for a minute anyone as low and lacking of intelligence as that boy could have taken my daughter and kept her hidden for eight days. He would have left a trail a mile wide.'

Slim nodded. 'Detective Reeves felt the same,' Slim said, unwilling to refer to the policeman in an informal manner. 'However, I still feel he might have something more to offer. Detective Reeves said he had been involved in certain escapades. During the course of such ... adventures, he might have seen something else. Do you know where I might find him?'

Georgia shrugged. 'Just hold your nose in the air and follow the dirtiest smell.'

～

Bernadette was waiting on their regular bench, eating a Mars bar and reading a tatty science-fiction book. Slim was pleased to see there were no fresh bruises on her face, and Bernadette actually smiled as he called out to her. She shifted across on the bench to allow him to sit down.

'Caught him yet?' she asked by way of greeting.

Slim shook his head. 'At present, I have no idea. However, I've uncovered a lot more questions, and that's usually a good place to start. How was school?'

'I wanted to burn it down. I resisted. I think you're having a positive effect on me. Look at this.' She held up the book, an old edition of Larry Niven's *Ringworld*. 'I didn't steal this. I got it from the library.'

'Do you have a card?'

Bernadette shrugged. 'No, but I'll definitely put it back.' She smiled. 'It's not that good.'

'I wouldn't know. I rarely read farther than the newspaper, and only if I'm forced to.'

'I suppose you get other people to do your donkey work.'

Slim shrugged. 'It comes with the celebrity.'

'Did you ever bribe anyone in prison?'

Slim laughed. 'No.'

'Not for cigarettes or drugs or anything?'

'I don't smoke—not anymore—and my poison was always the booze.'

'How does it feel to be an alcoholic? I mean, some people love to get hammered every day.'

'You really want to know?'

'Of course.'

Slim frowned. The feelings had always been with him, but he could never remember a time he'd had to put them into words.

'In a sense, wretched. It's not about getting hammered. It's about maintaining your sanity. The urge to drink … it's like arms pulling you in, and you're too weak to resist. And you know you're going to hate it and regret it but you can't pull away. You think "I'll just have one, then I'll stop and I'll go home" … but you never can. You drink until you run out or you pass out or someone punches you asleep and then you wake up and you feel like hell. And the first feeling is regret. You wonder where you've been and what you've done ... whose life you've ruined, whether the police are after you ... and you get up and you go into your kitchen to get a drink and you wonder if you've got anything left in the fridge, something to take the edge off how bad you feel ... and the cycle begins again.'

'Like a Ringworld,' Bernadette said.

Slim smiled. 'I'll let you interview me for the school magazine or whatever when I'm done with this case.'

'What's the worst thing you've ever done?'

'What?'

'While drunk.' Bernadette held up a plastic file. 'Go on, tell me. I'll trade for what I found online.'

Slim sighed. 'I drank a bottle of cheap whisky and tried to kill a man with a razor blade. Luckily for both of us, I was drunk enough to miss and he was sober enough to knock me out.'

'That's messed up. Did you regret it afterwards?'

Slim grimaced. 'Yes. But only because it was the wrong man.'

'Woah. Who would have been the right man?'

'A butcher called Mr Stiles. The man who was sleeping with my wife. The wife who, incidentally, faked my signature and aborted our child.'

'Christ,' Bernadette said. 'No wonder you drink. Your life's nearly as screwed up as mine. You've just done more miles.'

'And you're young enough to turn back.'

'Why do people call you Slim?'

Slim laughed. 'Enough questions. The answer to that is nowhere near as interesting anyway. So, what did you find out?'

Bernadette handed over the plastic file. 'Police reports,'

she said. 'Classified ones.'

'I was shown the official ones yesterday by a copper still working the case. They might be the same.'

'Bernadette shook her head. 'No, these were deleted files.'

'How do you know?'

'Because my source said so.'

Slim smiled. If Bernadette was playing a game, it didn't matter. The girl looked animated in a way he had never seen before. Whether she was helping or not wasn't the most important thing. It was doing her good.

'Okay, show me.'

'Right.' Bernadette reached across Slim and pulled the clusters of paper out of the file before handing them back to him. 'Copies of Emily's Year Nine exam papers,' she said. 'She took these tests just a couple of weeks before her disappearance.'

'Right.' Slim frowned. 'And how well did she do?' He flicked through the pages, but it had been so long since his own schooldays that the format was unfamiliar.

'She flunked,' Bernadette said. 'Look at this one. Maths. She answered the first nine questions. Out of a hundred. Then just stopped. Here, this is science. Six questions.' She pulled out another sheet. 'English. She didn't bother to answer. History, she only wrote her first name. But check this out. Art.'

Bernadette reclaimed the tests from Slim and fumbled through them, pulling out the last page. It was a bad photocopy of a scrawled pencil drawing.

'Is that not messed up?'

Slim squinted. 'It's a rock?'

Bernadette let out a cackling laugh that was almost triumphant. 'No, you idiot. It's a grave stone. And look: she's written her parents' names on it.'

19

Bernadette said she knew Julian Carter. He sold weed to her dad. Slim, still stunned by the photocopies of Emily's most recent tests, thanked Bernadette then headed into town to catch his bus to Tavistock.

As the bus trundled through the countryside on the border between Devon and Cornwall, Slim stared unseeing out of the window. What could it all mean? Emily had always been a studious pupil, according to everyone Slim had spoken with. No particular problems, consistent if unspectacular results. That it appeared she had intentionally failed the last set of testing prior to her disappearance—particularly considering that she later passed her GCSEs—suggested she had known something was about to happen.

Something else was bothering Slim too.

The writing on the crudely drawn gravestone was hard to decipher, but could be read as James and Georgia once someone had pointed it out. Between them, however, and slightly lower, appeared to be another word. Barely legible, Slim doubted it would have been clear to read even on the original drawing, as though it had been written in a way to be obvious only to Emily herself. It ought to read the girl's own name, but the shape of the letters had none of the consistency.

As he walked up the street from the bus stop in the direction of the community centre, he pulled out his phone and made a call.

'Kay?'

'Slim? Is that you?' Kay Skelton, a forensic linguist Slim had known in the army, laughed. 'Jesus, I wondered where you'd gone.'

'Wherever it was, eventually I came back. Listen, Kay, I don't have much time to talk. I need something deciphered. A word, or maybe a phrase, from a drawing. It seems deliberately illegible, but I think it meant something to the artist. I'm afraid I only have a copy, not the original.'

'Send me the best version you can get. A fax probably won't work, but if you can scan it, that might be okay. I can take a look at least.'

'Thanks, Kay. I can give you some information as to what it might say—'

'Hold that for a while. It's better if I go in blind, with an open mind. If I need help, I'll let you know.'

'Sure.'

Slim hung up. Just ahead, the lights of the community centre beckoned him. He was barely on time, filing in through the doors with the last of the stragglers. He was new in tonight's class also, so had to go through the same introduction at the beginning. He made a point of not looking at Emily, even though from the corner of his eye he noticed that unlike most of the students, she didn't look back.

She remained head down, scribbling into her

notebook, a polar opposite of the girl who, two years ago, had intentionally flunked a series of exams.

The lesson began, with Slim taking a seat near the back as he had before. He wondered now as he sat and tried to make sense of the teacher's words whether he should have taken a place closer to Emily, in an attempt to see what she was writing, but the girl had left a clear ring around herself which Slim couldn't infiltrate without making his intentions obvious.

He waited until the break between classes, but as before Emily took a position near to the window and peered out into the dark. Slim bought a coffee and wandered back towards the classrooms, hoping to get a glance at the work left on Emily's desk, but the teacher had locked the classroom door. Frustrated, he was forced to wait until the class resumed.

About midway through the lesson, with the coffee having taken both its positive and negative effects, Slim realised the obvious answer was staring him in the face. He stuck up a hand, requested to excuse himself, then quickly headed for the door at the front side of the room rather than the one nearer to him at the back. He got within a couple of strides before Emily became aware of him and pulled her work in close as though afraid he would copy her test scores. As the scattered documents were gathered, however, Slim caught a brief glimpse just before he was past her and pushing out of the door into the corridor.

He saw nothing specific. What was certain, though, was that the pages of scrawled pencil drawings had nothing to do with A-level geography.

20

He returned late to the Martins' place, frustrated. His attempt to photograph the number plate of the car collecting Emily had failed when the car took a different route to the previous one. The part of Slim's psyche which catered to paranoia wanted to believe he had been discovered, but the rational part gave itself to more simple explanations: a late night chip shop or DVD store run, a preference for a certain route, a preference for a change. There was no way of knowing, but he had to wait a few days now before he could chance it again.

He went into the kitchen and made himself coffee, certain he would find sleep hard to come by. The lights were off leading upstairs, meaning James and Georgia were already in bed. Slim closed the door to the hall and sat at the dining table, looking around the open-plan living room. He had sat here for a while most days, and found the over-sanitation frustrating. The Martins lived a clutter-free life. Everything was in its proper position, with nothing left lying around, and a complete absence of dust as though Georgia cleaned daily. It felt like a showroom. Even

Eight Days

the family photographs were specifically chosen, as though each image of family life had been carefully selected. Around the television stood a select few framed photographs, but each one was posed, as though taken professionally. James and Georgia with a newborn, Georgia with a beaming smile, James looking somewhat confused. Emily as a little girl, leaning on a bicycle. Georgia, now unsmiling, sitting on a wicker chair while an Emily of eight or nine stood in front. A more recent picture of Emily in her early teens had the family leaning against a vintage car. Only James was smiling in this one, while Emily, her hair perfectly straight, stared into the camera. Georgia, also unsmiling, had a faraway look in her eyes, as though something beyond the camera was far more interesting.

Wondering how he'd let himself get entangled in such a clearly dysfunctional family, Slim stood up and went to take a closer look at the picture. He set down a pen along its front edge then picked it up, turning it over. It had a sticker on the rear of a local photographer. Slim recognised the street name and wondered if it wouldn't be of interest to pay the photographer a visit. He had very little information on how the Martins behaved as a family, and while it might have no bearing whatsoever, friction between Emily and her parents could have been a contributor to Emily finding herself in a position of greater risk.

He put the picture down, being careful to align it exactly with the pen he had placed. Georgia appeared religiously organised, and while Slim felt sure she would allow him to view these pictures and more, he felt as though he were going behind her back by looking at them. Georgia had already proved herself to be a liar, and Slim's suspicion of her was growing daily. Could she have somehow been responsible for her own daughter's abduction?

There were famous cases, usually in an attempt at insurance fraud. It would certainly explain why Emily had gone to live with her grandparents, although it would therefore make it unlikely Georgia would have wanted his involvement. Slim had come across criminals in the past so confident that they'd hired him for a seemingly unsolvable investigation where they themselves were involved, but Georgia didn't come across that way. She seemed genuinely desperate to uncover the identity of her daughter's abductor.

The grandparents. Slim kept coming back to them. Georgia was still in denial, but neither she nor James had offered any direct way to make contact with the people supposedly in current charge of Emily's welfare.

It was something perhaps Slim needed to do by himself.

He finished the coffee and took the cup into the kitchen. Georgia had told him always to help himself, provided he cleaned up afterwards. Now, as he stared at the spotless sink, the tea towels hung in perfect lines, the edges of each side matching perfectly, the cups in the cupboard with their handles all turned to point the same way, he realised Georgia had a borderline case of OCD. Was that why she looked unhappy in many of the photographs? With the exception of the family shot with Emily as a baby, Georgia was unsmiling. Had her family failed to reach her expectations? What pressure had growing up in that environment placed on Emily?

He went upstairs to use the bathroom. Emily's room was at the end of the hall, the door closed. Slim couldn't resist taking another look, especially since the door to the Martins' bedroom was also closed.

Eight Days

He crept along the hall and opened the door. The first thing which struck him was that the curtains were pulled, allowing moonlight to flood into the room. The second was how clearly visible the field behind the house was, right up to the line of the trees. The gate he had climbed over was also visible. Partly hidden behind a neighbour's garden tree, it revealed itself each time the wind caused the branches to sway. As a car sped past, its lights bumping along the uneven lane, Slim could only wonder how haunting it might appear if someone were stood there, watching.

The gardens on either side both had tall rear hedgerows, grown to hide the field and the trees. Slim put a hand on the window frame and leaned close, trying to get a better look, wondering if perhaps the neighbours had also experienced Mrs Cleave and her nerve-shredding tales of the Woodland Man while growing up. In fact, the Martins' hedge appeared to have been kept low in general defiance.

Slim frowned, pulling his hand away. He had felt something under his fingers. A depression in the wood of the window frame, hidden by paint. He slid his hand along it, finding several others at random intervals.

They felt like nail holes, as though at one time this window had been boarded over.

He remembered Emily from the night classes, the way she had sat far away from the windows of the classroom, and then sat staring out of the window in the common area. Had she boarded the window shut herself, or had her parents done it for her?

Slim was considering how he might broach the subject with James as he stepped away from the window. A board creaked beneath his feet and a sudden rustling sound came from behind him. Slim spun, hands coming up, but there was no one there.

On the bed, however, visible above the mounded duvet Slim hadn't noticed on his way in, the moonlight illuminated the sleeping face of James.

21

'I got his number out of my dad's wallet,' Bernadette said, sounding proud. 'Dad was passed out drunk. He didn't notice.'

'How do you know it belongs to Carter?'

Bernadette rolled her eyes. 'Because I called it to make sure. Said I want some weed.' She smiled. 'Said I was sending a mate to get the stuff on my behalf. Told Carter he'd smell you before he saw you.'

'Thanks. What are you trying to say?'

Bernadette grinned. 'Didn't want him to think you were an undercover pig.'

'Just a real one?'

'No one would make themselves intentionally smell bad, would they?'

'I didn't realise I did.'

'Just your jacket. Perhaps it's time for a new one.'

Slim felt his cheeks redden, but if his old jacket served the purpose of putting Carter at ease, it was worth holding on to a while longer.

'Do you think you could do something else for me?' he asked.

'Yeah, whatever.'

'I'm trying to hunt down some of Emily's old friends. I want to know what they thought about her parents.'

'Do you think they were involved?'

'Right now I'm not sure what to think. Only that they seemed to have a complex relationship. The mother still seems to be in denial about it all, while the father has a very "never mind" attitude.'

'A what?'

'She doesn't live with them and hasn't for a while. They're deluding themselves that she'll be back any day. I was told she lived with her grandparents but I'm not sure about that.'

'Why would they lie?'

'I'm not convinced they are. At least, not the mother. I believe she genuinely thinks everything is all right. The father is just playing along for the sake of keeping the peace.'

'Why?'

Slim patted the bench between them. 'That's what I want you to find out. Right. I'd better get off. I have an errand to run before I meet Carter.'

He left her sitting on the bench and headed up through Coronation Park. It was a fine day and a few kids were sitting on the grass, studying or talking. As he reached the gates at the top, he passed a group of older boys smoking cigarettes. He was nearly through the gate when he heard a single muttered word.

'Perv.'

Slim paused. He waited a couple of seconds, then turned back. The boys had closed ranks, looking away from him. He waited until a couple glanced in his direction.

'Did someone say something?'

'Nah, mate,' one said, a tough guy taking exaggerated puffs on his cigarette. 'Think you need to clean your ears.'

'Or you're just going mental,' said another, as the rest of the group laughed.

Slim knew he ought to walk away, but he felt the same bloom of aggression which had occasionally got him in trouble during his military days.

'Maybe I am,' he said. 'You know, I was standing at my window last night, couldn't sleep. Saw some guy watching me. Had a little bird on his shoulder. Don't know what that was about. Anyone own a canary? Perhaps it was your dad.'

The boys shifted uncomfortably. A couple tossed their cigarettes to the ground and reached for their bags as if to leave. Others muttered expletives under their breath. The ringleader took a step forward.

'Why don't you get lost, old man?' he said. 'You're making the park look untidy.'

Slim met his gaze. 'If you hear the sound of a bird's chirping just behind your shoulder, don't ever turn around.'

From the look in their eyes, Slim knew they had heard the story. A couple more told him where to go in no uncertain terms, so he took his leave, heading through the gates and down the hill. As soon as he was out of their sight the shackles came off, and he heard them loudly berating him. A couple of rocks thrown over the hedge landed nearby, and Slim hastened out of range.

His meeting with Julian Carter was due to take place at Newport Industrial Estate, behind a builder's merchant, but he had another appointment first.

On Windmill Hill, a short distance down from the entrance to Coronation Park, Slim entered the gate of Launceston County Primary School and followed the signs to reception.

There, a secretary showed him to a seat where he waited until a door opened and a young woman looked through.

'Mr. Hardy?'

'Yes.'

The woman pushed spectacles up her nose and smiled as she offered him a hand. 'I'm Lisa May. I'm pleased to meet you.'

She had all the appearance of a dedicated teacher. Hair pulled into a bun. No make-up. A palm that felt hardworked. Clothes that could have been handmade. Slim saw the honesty in her eyes and decided he could trust her with his. As she led him down a corridor and into a bright, colourful classroom, he gave her a brief overview.

'A private investigator,' she said. 'That sounds exciting.'

'It has its moments,' Slim said. 'A large percentage of your time gets spent on paperwork you can't afford to hire staff for. And most cases aren't even criminal. Lots of extra-marital affairs, that kind of thing.'

'I imagine it's a break from the norm,' Lisa said. 'And nice not to have a routine.'

Slim forced a smile. Both normality and some form of routine were things he had hoped for from the Emily Martin case, but he had got neither, and things looked to be worsening by the day.

'It's a job which keeps you thinking,' he said.

Lisa led him through a side door into a narrow room which backed onto her classroom. A desk was crammed into a corner, surrounded by overflowing drawers and shelves.

Eight Days

'My respite from the madness,' Lisa said, spreading her hands. 'What little I can get. You asked about Emily Martin?'

'Yes.' Slim briefly explained about the drawings on the blog. Lisa nodded.

'I do something similar every year,' she said. 'Old Mrs Cleave had no idea what she was doing telling that awful story. It screwed up an entire generation. Of course, she's no longer around to see what damage her story did. We were left to pick up the pieces.'

'How so?'

'The Woodland Man is a favourite of bullies. It seems to pass from one generation of idiots to the next, no different to how we might pass on recipes for sponge cake to our kids. I doubt if many have a clue about the story's origins, but they all seem to find it somewhere. All that rubbish about a deformed guy in the woods, a canary on his shoulder.' She sighed. 'If the story was real, they'd all be his victims.'

'Did you hear it first-hand?'

Lisa May laughed. 'Oh dear, do I look so old? No, I heard it from my mother, who passed through Mrs Cleave's class. When I saw some children were still telling it, usually as a way of upsetting each other, I decided to do my own take on it to try to lighten the story up a little.'

'So you turned it into a kind of Harvest Festival symbol?'

'In a sense, although more of a summer solstice one. My version of the Woodland Man comes to urge on the growth of the summer crops, and to bless those who help to conserve his forests. It was a lot for kids of that age to accept, considering the conflicting stories they would hear in the playground, but if I saved just a couple from misery, it was worth every moment of my time.'

'I saw the displays, and I told you over the phone what I was after. Were you able to locate it?'

Lisa gave a grim nod. 'I'm afraid so, yes. I had hoped I'd thrown away the horrible thing, but it was there in the odds and sods drawer with all the other things kids haven't taken home over the years. I usually throw that stuff out every couple of years but I suppose I kept it as a curio. Hang on a moment. I'll fetch it.'

She went over to a wide chest of thin metal drawers, the like to hold artworks. From the bottom drawer she took something wrapped in a plastic bag and brought it over.

'How was Emily Martin as a child?' Slim asked, as Lisa sat down and began picking at a piece of tape fastening the plastic opening together.

Lisa gave a long 'hmmm' Slim could imagine her using towards difficult children. She frowned and brushed a strand of hair out of her eyes.

'In a word? Frustrating. I've worked with some pretty disturbed kids, and while she wasn't the worst by a long shot, she definitely had issues.'

'What kind?'

'Depressive, for the most part. She would go into these slumps that lasted for days sometimes. She'd do little other than stare at her desk. I'd be on the verge of calling social services when she'd suddenly snap out of it and she'd be fine for a few weeks afterwards.'

'You mentioned calling social services? Are you suggesting her issues were caused by her parents?'

Lisa shook her head. 'Not her parents. Just her mother.'

22

'Oh, I know she comes across as a nice-as-pie, butter-wouldn't-melt type, but she's far different under the surface. A closed-doors dragon.'

'You think she was abusing Emily?'

Lisa shook her head. 'Not in the traditional sense. The girl never had a mark on her. She was well fed, always had nice clothes, and her school kit was always good. She smelled clean too. No, it was more complicated than that, difficult to identify.' Lisa gave a tired shrug and for a moment her eyes looked weepy. Then she shook it away, forcing a smile.

'My own mother was much the same,' she said. 'That's how I knew. Nothing you do is ever right, no achievement is ever good enough. Children grow up with a need to be praised, to impress their parents, and if every achievement is lambasted or denigrated, they quickly develop a sense of disillusionment. They go the opposite way, either outwardly into rebellion, or inwardly into depression.'

'You don't appear to be the type,' Slim said.

Lisa looked up at him and for a moment her eyes

hardened. A different person stared back, one long suppressed.

'I set fire to my school at the age of fourteen,' she said. 'A teacher nearly died. I was lucky to escape with a juvenile sentence. I was in that place for three years, and during that time my mother didn't visit a single time. In hindsight it was the best thing for me. My mother all but cut me off. These days I get the occasional Christmas card, but that's about it. Still, free from her clutches, I straightened my life out.' She spread her arms and smiled as though to emphasize the point.

'Good for you. And I suppose when you saw Emily, you understood what she was going through?'

Lisa nodded. 'Other teachers had passed on information on her class performance, as is normal, but I spotted the signs as soon as she came into my class. She would try really hard on something until it went home, then she'd be down for days afterwards. She was receiving none of the praise required by children at that high development stage. Certainly not from her mother.'

'Did you meet Georgia Martin?'

'Oh yes, she was always there at parents' evenings. She always wanted to know how her daughter was progressing. On the outside she was fine, but I could see the perfectionist in her eyes. She expected too much from Emily. She wanted her daughter to be perfect, hence the operations. And that was never going to happen, was it?'

'What operations?'

'You didn't know? They tried to fix her vocal chords. She was often out of school, sent to see specialists, given keyhole surgery I'm guessing the Martins paid for, considering the lack of effectiveness. I felt so sorry for the poor girl, with the constant upheaval. She was perfect just the way she was, but that was never going to be enough for her mother.'

'I was under the impression she had a condition that couldn't be fixed.'

'That didn't stop her mother trying.' Lisa had managed to unseal the plastic bag covering the picture and slid it out, placing it on the table in front of Slim. 'Children often express themselves in art. My instructions were to draw a picture of the Woodland Man, welcoming him to our school. The pupils sat by the classroom window and painted their interpretations of the school field with the Woodland Man coming towards the school.' She patted the picture. 'And this monstrosity is what Emily painted. It, um, fails somewhat to express what I'd expected, and was unsuitable for the display. I told Emily I'd spilt a jar of paintbrush water on it.' Lisa brushed the same strand of hair out of her face. Slim could tell from the way her cheeks had flushed and her eyes darted around that the memory of what she had done still haunted her. 'I made a real show of it, crying and everything,' she continued as her eyes welled up all over again. 'The poor girl looked so disappointed, but as you can see it's wholly inappropriate, and I also didn't want her taking it home to her parents. God knows what childhood memory this comes from.'

Slim stared at the painting. It was remarkably good for a child of ten, with correct perspective and a clarity in the images which left no doubt as to what they were meant to portray.

The field looked like the one he had seen from the classroom window, only with taller trees along the back hedge and a line of houses to the left which were now hidden by a hedge that had grown up in the intervening years.

'I think it represents how Emily felt perceived by her

mother,' Lisa said. 'I meant to throw it away, I just never got around to it. There's something I don't like about throwing away a pupil's work, and it does have a certain ... merit.'

Slim stared at the image in the centre. Standing about halfway across the playground was a female figure. She had long black hair and spots of blue for eyes. A red, upward curving strip for a mouth.

The figure alone would have been agreeable, an interpretation that the Woodland Man was in fact female. The figure beside it defied all of that however.

The woman's arms stretched out to the side, where she was holding the handle of a pram. The pram, standing side on, had a cover pushed back, and the child was standing up, arms raised over its head.

Its eyes were dots of red and its teeth jagged slashes of black.

23

The ascent down the steep hill past the castle had left Slim's knees aching. Newport Industrial Estate was found in the valley between Launceston and Newport, alongside a river. On the estate was a builder's merchant, a couple of DIY shops, a chippy, and a pet shop. It was also where the main station for the Launceston Railway was found, a pretty tourist train ride along the valley and back. As he passed the entrance, Slim wished he had time for something so relaxing, but he was late for his meeting with Carter.

He circled behind the builder's merchant and climbed into the weeds around the back, where Bernadette had told him to wait for Carter. Here he found evidence of other nefarious deeds: several crushed beer cans, a discarded syringe, a couple of ragged magazines. He stepped carefully over them as he paced up and down through the weeds.

At one point he heard a vehicle pull up around the side, so he peered out, watching an open-backed truck with an awning over its contents reversing into position near a rear door. A man got out, came around the back, and pulled the awning off. Slim saw lines of buckets in the back, thirty or forty. The man began to lift them down and carry them into the warehouse. On one journey he tripped, spilling grey sand on the ground, then swore and kicked it into the weeds. Slim watched him, then turned away, right into the face of a grinning man with wild, psychotic eyes.

'Johnny?'

Slim almost forgot his assumed name. 'Yes.'

'Julian. How much gear you after?'

Slim was still recovering from the shock of finding Carter so close he could have put a knife in Slim's back. He eased away out of stabbing range, silently berating himself for letting his guard down, while Carter stared at him, a crazed grin displaying several missing teeth. How this lunatic could have been sleeping with a doctor's wife Slim couldn't fathom, but perhaps the doctor was of such failed attractiveness that even a ghoul like Carter was desirable.

Slim made a deal for a small amount of weed and reached into his pocket for some cash.

'You came all the way down here just for that?' Carter said.

'I'm a beginner.' Slim pulled out his hand, fist closed. 'And actually, I wanted to ask you something.'

'What?'

'It's nothing much. It'll only take a minute.'

'Nah, screw this.'

Carter started to back away, but Slim had been readying himself. He moved forward, ducking low as Carter swung a wild punch, dropping a shoulder in towards Carter's chest and bringing himself up inside the younger man's body. He hooked his left arm over Carter's right, then spun him around, pushing him up against the warehouse wall.

'What is this? A bust?' Carter gasped, his wild eyes staring. 'I knew that cow was lying—'

'It's nothing,' Slim said. 'I'm no better than you. I just got out of the slammer and I'm trying to get my life back on track.'

'What the hell do you want? Get off me.'

'Information, that's all. I want to know about Emily Martin.'

'What? Emily? What are you talking about?'

'You knew her. I know you did. You used to run across the field behind her house, visiting someone, but you saw her, didn't you? A young girl in her room. What was she doing? Getting changed?'

Carter struggled, but Slim held him tight.

'Talk, Julian. No one knows we're here. I'm ex-military. I could make this very bad for you.'

'I never ... I didn't ... it was that doctor's wife. She was getting me stuff to cut. Proper grade stuff.'

'And you were selling her a good time in return?'

'He wasn't interested, whatever. She was pretty old, but it wasn't so bad if I'd had a hit of something.'

'How nice for you. Tell me about Emily Martin. Did you know her? Did you see her?'

Carter groaned as Slim squeezed tighter. 'Once or twice, that's all. Once or twice before and a couple of times after.'

'Doing what?'

'Nothing. Sitting there by the window like bloody Juliet. Staring out at the field. I thought she saw me a couple of times at night because she'd jump up and whip the curtains shut, but I lay down in the grass a while and she'd open them up again. She was waiting for someone.'

'Did you ever see who?'

'Nah, man, not my business. Had my own piece waiting I had to deal with. I'm not some pedo. I have no interest in little girls.'

'You said you saw her after?'

'Yeah, once, maybe twice. I was curious then, see. After she got nabbed and then showed up. Walked past there one night and she's there by the window as before. Might have seen her again, don't remember. Next time I do remember, though, it's not her, but her mother. And I didn't see her for long.'

'Why not?'

'Because she was in there nailing boards up over the window.'

24

Slim pushed Carter to the ground, then reached into his pocket. As Carter twisted around, Slim grabbed his hand, but this time he thrust two hundred quid in used ten pound notes into Carter's fingers, then squeezed them shut. He pushed Carter's hand away, noticed the man's incredulous look, and smiled.

'That's for your trouble,' he said. 'And I'm sorry about strong-arming you. Really. I prefer it to running, but sometimes I need things said.'

'Watch your back,' Carter snarled as he backed away, the money swiftly pocketed, but it was the retort of a wounded, retreating beast, beaten in battle but relieved to be escaping with its life. 'I'll be looking for you, old man.'

'Line those banknotes up by serial number and you'll find my phone,' Slim said, having written the digits of his number across several of the notes. 'In case you remember anything else. There's the same again in it for you, and I promise not to rough you up next time.'

It was a modest olive branch, one designed to soften the pain of defeat and relax feelings of revenge. It was unlikely Carter had more to tell, and even more unlikely he had the patience to figure out Slim's number, but Launceston was a small town and Carter certainly had more friends than he did. Someone might know something.

He took a scenic route back up the hill and past the castle, making sure to avoid bumping into Carter again so soon.

His head was starting to ache with ideas and possibilities. Nothing made much sense, but at least he had some leads to go on. The more he thought about it, the harder he found it to turn his suspicions away from the family themselves. Georgia, in particular, had an under layer he was just starting to uncover. Psychopaths came in all shapes and sizes, but he still found it hard to believe that she could have been involved in her daughter's disappearance. If she had something to hide, why would she have hired him?

He needed some answers and explanations if he was ever going to get anywhere, however. Georgia was a book he didn't dare open, so that left James. Gaining the man's trust was paramount, but there was also the fear that he might pass information onto his wife.

By the time Slim got back to the house, the Martins had finished dinner already. Georgia had saved Slim some casserole and set him a place at the table despite his protestations that a bowl eaten alone in his room would suffice. It was still light outside so James was pottering about in the garden. As Georgia served Slim's food up on a tray and carried it through to the dining room, Slim watched her husband crouched over a flowerbed at the end of the garden where he appeared to be pulling up weeds.

'Mr Hardy, your supper's ready,' Georgia called. Slim took one last look at James before starting to eat.

Eight Days

∽

'The views are spectacular,' James said. 'We ought to come up here more often, if truth be told.'

Slim paused to catch his breath, watching James trudge through the grass ahead. In the distance, a stack of pebble-shaped rocks the size of a house marked their eventual destination.

Dartmoor as a destination for a quiet chat sounded great on paper, but Slim was dangerously out of shape and feeling every step. James clearly took a lot more exercise than his frame suggested, and was setting a pace Slim struggled to maintain.

He was on the verge of giving up and heading back to the car park when James called a halt. The older man sat down on a rock and pulled a flask out of his bag.

'You picked a great day,' he said, as Slim slumped down beside him. 'Been years since I've been up here. It's so lovely, isn't it?'

Slim, still getting his breath back, grunted.

'How's the investigation? You haven't said much about your progress of late.'

James bringing up the subject had saved Slim the bother of doing so. He waited until he could speak without difficulty, then said, 'It's not going as well as I'd like. Every lead I get sends me off on another tangent. It doesn't help that I'm not being given all the available information.'

'I'll tell Graham to make sure you get more time with—'

'It's not him,' Slim said, his exhaustion stripping him of patience as well as breath. 'I don't believe you or Georgia are being straight with me.'

'What on earth do you mean?'

Slim had meant to take his time getting to the point, but he decided to just lay it down.

'Why didn't you tell me she was unable to speak? All this time I've been wondering why she wouldn't talk to anyone, and I find out from her school friends that she was clinically mute.'

'Mute? I wouldn't call it that.'

'What then?'

'Well, Georgia just liked to say she was quiet. And of course Emily was, but over the years you develop a way of communicating, of understanding what sounds she can make and their meanings, and after a while you just forget.'

Slim grimaced. With no experience as a parent, he decided to keep his comments relevant to the investigation.

'Did you develop any other way of communicating? Sign language, for example?'

James shook his head. 'Georgia forbade it. She didn't want Emily to grow up with an understanding that she was disadvantaged.'

'So she forbade her a way to communicate? You have to be joking.'

James gave an embarrassed shrug. 'I believe the primary school gave her special classes against our wishes, so she understood the basics.'

'Why would such classes be against your wishes? Or do you mean Georgia's wishes?'

'Look, Mr. Hardy—Slim—... I'm not sure where you're leading with this, but—'

Slim put up a hand. 'One more question. Answer me truthfully or I'm done with this investigation. Is Emily really living with your parents in Tavistock, like you told me, or is that just a line you spun me?'

Eight Days

James winced. 'Look, I wasn't sure what to say ... I didn't know what you might say to Georgia—'

'Just tell me, James.'

With a long sigh, James shook his head. 'My parents are both in a nursing home near Plymouth.'

'Then who is she living with?'

'No one. She was legally an adult at sixteen so she moved out. As far as I know, she lives alone.'

25

'I BELIEVE SHE LIVES IN A COUNCIL FLAT,' JAMES SAID. 'She always liked Tavistock, because it had some good art shops, I believe. She registered as homeless with the council and they found her a place. I believe she works in a local craft shop while going to night classes for her A-levels, but I'm not sure.'

'And you have no contact with her?'

James shrugged. 'None directly. I have a friend living in Tavistock who keeps an eye on her. And I've been to see her a couple of times, even though she was reluctant to talk to me. She has no intention of coming home.'

'Because of Georgia?'

James sighed. 'They had the usual mother and teenage daughter squabbles. Then the abduction happened, and after that they were distant. They didn't really communicate at all. Even less than before.'

Slim paused before asking his next question. James had opened up at last, but he feared pushing the man too far. While he had threatened it, he didn't want to drop the investigation, because he needed the Martins' money. And for the same reason, he was reluctant to push his suspicions of Georgia even further.

'My wife, she's a complicated woman,' James said suddenly, filling in the air space. 'She's very much from an older generation, one obsessed with keeping up appearances. It hurts her a lot to admit failings in anything. Sometimes it's easier to go along with things than to challenge them. With all due respect, Slim, I don't believe your investigation is necessary. I was against hiring you from the start, but Georgia is determined to find out who took Emily. Personally, I don't think she'll ever know, because the police would have found out, wouldn't they, if there was enough of a trail to follow. And after all, Emily came back to us. It might take a few years of healing to get things back to normal, but dredging up the past can only cause more pain.'

Slim slowly turned to face James, who was sitting beside him, a plastic cup half full of coffee clutched in both hands as though it were the only point of warmth left in the world.

'You said "she'll never know", not "we'll", James. Be honest with me, even if you're not prepared to give me a name. Do you know who took your daughter?'

He watched James's response carefully, but all James did was sigh. A flinch or a hurried response might have suggested guilt, but James just gave a slow shake of his head.

'It was a slip of the tongue. Unlike Georgia, I'm at peace with not knowing,' he said. 'If the police couldn't figure it out, and you can't, and if Emily genuinely doesn't know, then I don't think we'll ever find out.'

'And that doesn't bother you?'

James shrugged and smiled. 'Well, not really. If the abductor was as bad as all that, they wouldn't have brought her back. I think perhaps we should all move on. Things are what they are, and we can't change them now, can we?'

~

James dropped Slim off at home, then immediately said he needed to pick something up from a friend. Slim watched him drive away before heading up to the house. Georgia didn't answer when he rang the bell, so he let himself in with a key they had given to him.

He had been most looking forward to a strong coffee, but a quick search established Georgia was out. Taking advantage of a few moments in the house alone, Slim headed upstairs to Emily's room.

It was as he remembered it, tidy, untouched, the bed neatly made. He had lost nerve when it came to asking James why he had been sleeping in here, so he logged it for the next opportunity.

He went to the window and peered out, aware anyone in the field could see him, but there was no one by the gate or under the trees, or down by the row of houses along the right where the doctor's wife Julian Carter had been sleeping with supposedly lived. Slim stared at the view for a long time, some sense of awareness growing in his mind but failing to make itself known.

Finally, he turned away, and began a search of the room's secret places. The drawers and cupboards were empty, as he had expected. One by one he pulled out the drawers and turned them over, looking for something fixed to the underside, but found nothing. On one he found a slight area of tape residue, but whatever might have been hidden there was long gone.

Next he turned his attention to the bed, lifting the sheets and mattress, examining the edges of the box bottom, looking for something that had been hidden. This time he found a spot near the foot by the wall where the mattress had been cut open and then stitched back up, but whatever had been hidden inside had been retrieved. Slim used a pen to stretch a hole between two stitches and then poked a finger inside. It came away a little dusty, so he wiped it on a handkerchief and folded it carefully before putting it into his pocket. It might be something, or it might not.

After giving up on the bed, he got to work on the desk, pulling it out from the wall and examining every surface. This time he had better luck. On the back leg, written in a descending line, were a series of numbers. Someone had tried to erase them, but if Slim angled the desk towards the window the light caught the depressions on the wood. He wrote them down, then slid the desk back into place, careful to put the legs back into the exact carpet depressions they had been in before.

He had just stood up when the front door opened downstairs, a creak of hinges giving the entrant away. Slim gathered his thoughts and planned an escape route into the upstairs bathroom, just as he realised from the view outside what he had been missing. He stared for a moment, giving a little shake of the head, then hastened to get out of the room before his intrusion was discovered.

26

Bernadette wasn't on the bench where he had expected to find her. Monday afternoon had seen the onset of a drizzle threatened from the morning, so he wasn't surprised, but he did a circuit of the pond through the trees in case she was sheltering somewhere, then took a look inside the leisure centre. The girl wasn't in the same customer waiting area, so Slim guessed he had either missed her or upset her somehow.

He stood in the rain for a while with an umbrella over his head, but Bernadette never appeared along the path the pupils took when leaving Launceston College. He spotted a couple of the boys who had berated him as they moved up the hill, so he turned away and stepped back into a stand of trees until they were out of sight.

Still no Bernadette. Giving up, Slim walked through Coronation Park and down into the town where he caught a bus heading over to Newport. He got off near the estate and walked to Dave Brockhill's house. Slim had hoped to ask the former teacher about his days as the local netball coach, but it appeared Brockhill wasn't home. A side gate

Eight Days

was open, so Slim, not wanting to waste the journey, went around the back to make sure.

He found himself in a neat garden. Potted plants gathered on a patio which led down to a tidy square of lawn which itself ended in an area of sand and stones punctuated by small fruit trees.

Slim frowned. Still frowning, he took a walk across the lawn to the tree area. The sand was coarse, ungraded as though it had been shovelled from a beach. Instinctively he scooped up a handful and put it into his pocket, before flattening the disturbed area with the toe of his shoe.

Heading back around the side, he noticed a couple of bags of sand perhaps left over from Brockhill's landscaping project. One was unopened, the other sealed by a plastic clip. Both had the logo of the builder's merchant on Newport Industrial Estate.

Slim remembered the truck he had seen unloading buckets of sand. Was it possible the trader was cutting beach sand with its own to make an extra profit?

He decided not to wait around for Dave Brockhill, instead heading down the hill to the estate. Acting like a regular customer, he went into the builder's merchant and browsed the goods for sale. When one sales assistant asked him what he was after, he enquired on the best way to lay a patio.

With a firm sand base, he was told. Enquiring about materials, he was led to the sand section, and advised the store's own brand was both the cheapest and most effective, because of its composite make-up. Slim thanked the man and left.

Evening had arrived without warning. His phone battery was nearly dead, so he found a phone box and called Kay.

Any news on that picture?' he asked.

'Working on it,' Kay said. 'I need a day or two more.'

'I have a couple of other things you might be able to help me with. I need some tests done.'

'You know I only deal with linguistics, Slim.'

'Sure, but you forensics types all stick together. Don't you have a favour or two you could cash in?'

Kay laughed. 'Slim, I've cashed in enough favours for you to last a lifetime.'

Slim paused, allowing Kay to talk himself around.

'But since it's never anything dull, I'll see what I can do. What is it?'

'Two incredibly dull things,' Slim said. 'I need a dust sample checked. I think it might contain drug residue. And I need two handfuls of sand analysed to see if they come from the same source.'

Kay laughed again. 'Dull on the outside, but nothing with you is ever dull on the inside. Courier them to me and I'll see what I can do.'

'Thanks.'

Next, Slim called Donald Lane.

'Don, it's Slim. I need something else looked into. I have a number, but I'm not sure what it's for. I thought it was for a phone, but if it is, it needs an area code and I don't know it. It could be something else, though. A serial number, perhaps.'

'Sure, let me know.'

Slim read off the list of numbers. 'One other thing. I wondered if you could get me a copy of Emily Martin's birth certificate. I want to contact the registrar who signed it off. Background research.'

'No problem. Just give me the parents' full names. You need an official reason to request one if you're not next of kin, but I'm pretty sure I can pull it off.'

'Thanks, Don, you're a legend.'

'An underpaid one, but I'm always happy to help. Look after yourself, Slim.'

'And you.'

Slim hung up. Daunted by the steep walk up through Launceston, and having missed the last bus, Slim headed for a greasy spoon cafe on the corner of the industrial estate to rest up and gather his thoughts. Ordering himself a burger and chips, he pulled his notebooks out of his bag and went over what he had discovered.

Dave Brockhill didn't come across as a kidnapper, and there was the eternal question of motive. Plus, if the composite of minerals in the sand at the builder's merchant matched what had been found between Emily Martin's toes, it only confirmed that a customer of the store may have been involved, and with a store so large there would be many. In addition, it was possible that Brockhill had put the feature in long after the kidnapping had taken place.

So many fingers of suspicion still pointed at Georgia. The woman came across as a closet control freak and narcissist, but if so, why hire him? Despite the prison sentence, these days Slim's name came with a certain reputation, and if Georgia was playing games she risked a lot. However, the case was a knot he couldn't yet unravel.

Emily. The girl was key. Slim needed to meet with her, and the risk of being rejected was worth the possible rewards.

Night had fallen outside. With a sigh and a grimace at the thought of the long walk back, Slim pushed himself up, shouldered his bag, and headed out.

He had barely stepped out of the cafe's front door when someone grabbed him from behind, dragging him backwards.

Too weary to muster the strength to resist, he was

dragged into an alley behind the greasy spoon, a hand over his mouth smelling faintly of salt. Someone else appeared in front of him, a balaclava over his face.

'Leave town and don't come back,' said a voice into his ear, then the first punch came in.

Slim, wearing his thick jacket over a sweater, fell to the ground, bunching his stomach muscles and holding his arms over his face as the blows rained down.

27

It had felt like minutes but in retrospect the attack had probably lasted no more than thirty seconds before his two attackers had bolted, fleeing shadows in the dark. Slim had watched them go, trying to retain some clue as to their identity, but the gloom and the background traffic noise had left him little.

The walk back to the Martins' place had been more tiring than usual, but the damage done by the mugging had been superfluous, the shock and fear worse than any of the punches or kicks. A warning only. They had avoided his face where marks could be seen, targeting his body, but his thick coat had protected him from any serious damage. As he stood in the Martins' shower with dawn glittering through the frosted window, he winced as he rubbed soap over welts and bruises, wishing he could take a day off.

Carter's revenge had come sooner than expected. Slim, however, knew he should have watched his back. Launceston was not a place where you could easily be lost.

Of course, he had no intention of doing what his attacker had ordered. He just needed to be more careful.

Georgia was pottering in the front garden, so Slim headed out, walking down the lane to the gate leading into the field behind the Martins' property. There, he called another old mate, the spiky Alan Coaker, requesting something to protect himself.

'I'll put a suit of armour in the next post,' Alan said gruffly. 'Don't scratch it. I want it returned.'

Slim muttered thanks, wondering how likely it was that Alan was joking. The hardware and security expert had sprung a few past surprises over the years, Slim remembered with a wry smile.

Aware that close to the hedge he would be hidden from the Martins' garden, Slim climbed over the gate into the field and walked around the perimeter until he was directly outside the Martins' property. The view here wasn't quite the same as from Emily's window, but it was close enough.

The basics of a child's painting had made him initially mistake a farmer's field for a school's sports field, but now that he looked at it, the differences were obvious. Emily had painted the houses to the left because the ones visible from her bedroom window were not obscured by trees like those partially seen from the Year Four classroom, while she had painted larger trees at the field's rear because in her painting they were supposed to be.

Emily had not painted the Woodland Man in the school playground, but in the field behind her house. And her Woodland Man had been a woman, pushing a monstrosity in a pram.

There had to be a specific reason why she had altered the location, and if she had altered the location because of what she had seen, then there had to be a reason why she had drawn a woman with a pram.

Slim hadn't taken a photograph of the picture, but it still haunted him. And if just an image of it made him feel so cold inside, how might Emily have felt to see the real thing?

He remembered how she had peered out of the window at the community centre as if waiting for something, and how she had sat so far away from it during class.

Something out in the dark was haunting her.

Could it be the same thing that had made her vanish for eight days?

The same person?

Not wanting to go back to the Martins' place, but it being too early to wait for Bernadette, Slim went back into town and headed for the library. There, he spent some time trawling the internet for any information he might have missed. Disappointed that the internet was for once proving of little use, he approached the librarian and asked where he might find books on local myths and legends.

Directed to a local history section, he flicked through half a dozen books before giving up. The Woodland Man, it seemed, existed only in spoken word stories.

Then he hit on another idea, and went online again, searching for old Mrs. Cleave's next of kin. She had no children it seemed, but he found a reference to a niece, a Norah Cleave, who lived not far from Launceston in a village called Calderstock.

Using an old-fashioned phone book, Slim was able to find an address and telephone number. He assumed his alter-ego Mike Lewis and called her, and to his surprise Norah Cleave's initial reluctance abruptly changed when he explained that he was researching for a BBC documentary on local myths and legends. Just after lunch, he caught a bus from the town centre which took him out on windy moorland roads into the effective middle of nowhere, leaving him at a bus stop at a crossroads of country lanes surrounded by trees and tall hedgerows.

Had it not been for the middle-aged woman sitting on a weed-entangled bench on the other side of the road, Slim would have been lost, but she stood up and waved, a wide smile on her face.

'Quick,' she said. 'They're about to let the hounds out.'

Slim jumped, glancing back over his shoulder, but the woman let out a loud guffaw and slapped her stomach. 'I'm playing. You've got city boy written all over you. Not many people come out into these wilds by choice, and I bet you BBC types rarely get outside London, do you? Don't worry, the kettle's hot. You're a coffee man, I gather?'

'How did you know?'

'You look tired.' She nodded her head in the direction of one of the forks in the road. 'Come on, it's this way. I've got something to wake you up.'

28

Norah Cleave lived alone in a ramshackle old farmhouse on a hillside surrounded by tall sycamore trees. Several padlocked outbuildings in various states of repair stood among trees and bushes Norah had likely let grow up in the years since the farm had been worked. The afternoon sun hung directly overhead, and with the background chatter of birds hidden among the tree branches, Slim felt a sense of solitude and peace unlike any he had felt in some time. From the extensive, overgrown gardens, no other local residences were visible, and when Slim enquired as to the location of the rest of Calderstock, Norah absently flapped a hand at the triangle of valley visible between two tall trees.

'What there is of it is down there. Not much reason for a visit. Doesn't even have a shop anymore, and now the parish council idiots who wouldn't use the old shop keep hassling me to volunteer in their pet community one. Gah. There's a reason I let the hedgerows grow up and put the *Beware of the Dog* sign up on the gate.'

'You don't have one?'

Norah smiled and lifted a fat tortoiseshell cat down off a kitchen counter. 'The cats would terrorise the poor thing.'

Slim had counted five so far, and among the gardens, in which he had spotted rockeries, water features, and concealed lawns, there were certainly more. Norah, it turned out, was a professional artist, and had gone out of her way to appear as crazy as possible.

'Unfortunately there's no pasture land left to go with the house,' Norah said. 'Only the yard. I use a few of those buildings for storage, one of the biggest ones as an art studio. My grandfather sold off all the fields to a neighbour decades ago. No money in farming these days. They only do it for the subsidies, but if they have any real sense they build golf courses and petting zoos, bring in the suits and the kids.'

'Your grandfather was Mrs. Cleave's brother?'

'My father. Lillian Cleave was my aunt. My father got married late. My mother was in her forties when I was born so they're both long gone. Get off of that.' With a sudden scowl she aimed a kick at a big tuxedo cat running its claws down a doorframe already scarred with claw marks. As the cat bolted, avoiding her slipper by a hair's width, Norah turned back to Slim, her smile returning.

'Neither of my parents were the most stable of people and the impression they left encouraged me to stay the hell away from relationships. I made the mistake a couple of times, but I learned my lesson in the end. Are you married, Mike?'

Almost forgetting the identity under which he had arrived, Slim said, 'Once. Biggest mistake of my life. She ran off with a cameraman.'

Norah laughed and spread her hands. 'See? Did you get a cat?'

Slim smiled. 'I'm a dog person.'

'No wonder the cats look nervous. They can tell, you know. They have a sixth sense.'

Slim looked at a fat tabby perched on a nearby tabletop, next to a large vase of dried flowers, which had been eyeing him like prey for several minutes. 'I don't doubt it,' he said.

Norah guffawed again as she handed him a mug of coffee. 'Right. You were asking about my aunt. Let's see what I can find.'

Norah led him through into a cluttered living room where she shifted a pile of books off an armchair to give him space to sit.

'After your call, I did hunt out a few bits and bobs,' she said. 'Take a seat. I need a minute or two to remember where I put them.'

A moment after she had gone into an adjacent room, the tortoiseshell claimed Slim's lap, leaving him no choice but to sip his coffee with one hand while petting the warm, purring beast with the other. The tabby, which had followed them, took up a position on a nearby chair from which to maintain its observation. Avoiding its suspicious glare, Slim looked out of a living room window into a glass conservatory filled with plants in hand-painted pots. A couple of plastic bags of animal feed stood near a door that opened to the outside. Around the living room, he wasn't surprised to spot no TV hidden among the piles of magazines, newspapers, and books. A couple of framed pictures stood among generic sculptures and other dusty antiques. One was of a young man in his early twenties with his arm around the shoulders of a slightly younger Norah, suggesting that one of her aforementioned failed relationships had resulted in a son.

Before Slim could adjust the cat on his lap enough to

look for any more personal mementoes, Norah returned with a wicker basket filled with bits of paper. She put it down on a coffee table, glanced at the resting cat and frowned. 'Lawrence likes visitors,' she said. 'Feel free to shift him if he's getting heavy. Benny over there is a little more standoffish.'

'I noticed,' Slim said, massaging Lawrence's neck as the cat arched its head towards him. 'Were you close to your aunt?'

Norah laughed. 'Hell no. Couldn't stand her. And no doubt she felt the same about me. Aunt Lillian was not a child person.'

'Teaching was perhaps an unusual choice of profession, then?'

'The way Dad always told it was that my grandfather insisted his children learn a trade. Dad was a local builder. Lillian went into teaching because it was a course available at the nearest college. She was a hard person, though. Ruled her pupils with an iron hand. I went to a different school but I always heard that Mrs. Cleave's class was a true rite of passage. You went into it full of innocence and joy for the world, and you came out of it hardened to life's miseries.'

'It sounds like she left a legacy.'

'You know how every school has a feared teacher, one that leaves a lasting memory? It was certainly her, and I wouldn't even know firsthand. Thankfully she never taught me. For a woman full of stories, she hated creativity in anyone else. I'd have ended up working in Tesco or something.'

'As I mentioned on the phone, I'm doing preliminary research for a documentary on local myths and legends. It was her story I most wanted to ask about. The Woodland Man.'

Eight Days

Norah gave a nervous, unsettled laugh. 'Another reason I planted those trees,' she said. 'I didn't like the view.'

'She told you the story?'

'That damn story ... she delighted in it. She babysat me once. God, I remember it like it was yesterday. She made me sit by the open curtains while she told me this supposed bedtime story. When she was done, she told me to go upstairs and pull my bedroom curtains tight. He'd climb right up and sit outside the window, she said. Sit there and listen for any moving about or talking when I was supposed to be in bed. And if I dared peek out through the curtains, I'd see his face right there, peering in at me. Scared the living daylights out of me. I went up to bed but I didn't sleep all night. I was so upset the next day that Dad might have said something to her. She certainly never babysat me again, but whenever we visited her, she would give me this cruel smile and a wink, just to remind me.'

'I heard a girl killed herself a few years after hearing the story. Susan something?'

Norah looked down at her hands. 'Susan Cole-Bridger. I remember.'

'Did you know her?'

Norah looked at the floor and gave a quick shake of her head. 'Only by name. I'd seen her around. We were about the same age.'

'Do you remember your aunt's reaction?'

Norah shook her head. 'I'd pretty much stopped having much contact with her by then, and as soon as I was done with school I moved to Exeter to go to college. I stayed there to work for another fifteen years, so Aunt Lillian was long retired by the time I came back to Cornwall. I only ever saw her a handful of times after that, but she lost her marbles quickly. She spent the last twenty years of her life in a care facility.' She sighed, slapping the seat of the chair for emphasis. 'She outlasted both my parents by a good ten years. I wondered if she would outlast me. It wouldn't have surprised me. The very last time I saw her, a courtesy visit about six months before she died, she still had that horrible gleam in her eyes. She no longer remembered my name, but she knew who I was, and how she had tormented me. And I know exactly how she must have felt when she heard about poor Susan.'

'And how's that?'

Norah gave a sad smile. 'Victorious.'

29

During the bus ride home, Slim struggled to get the images Norah Cleave had shown him out of his head. Lillian Cleave had seemingly never smiled. From black and white photographs of her as a child standing beside her brother to one modern photo of a wheelchair-bound elderly woman, she had worn that same hostile expression, an outward stare that suggested a general hatred for the world.

And what better place to invoke her hatred than a classroom? Slim could just imagine her looking up at the end of the story to see the children's horrified faces and feeling a deep, dark sense of satisfaction.

As he got off the bus in Launceston, he wondered if he was any closer to figuring out the mystery. All he had done was unearth further questions, some decades old.

He was too late to wait for Bernadette, but the aches from last night's beating appeared to have intensified, so he went into a cafe across the street and ordered a coffee. Sitting by the wall but with a view of the window, he watched people passing on the street outside as he thoughtfully sipped his coffee. He felt a little more confident than he had this time yesterday, after receiving an automated message from the local post office to say a package had arrived. It would surely be from Alan Coaker, and hopefully wouldn't be one of Alan's jokes. When asking for something to protect himself, it wasn't out of the question that Alan would send him an ornamental sword or a can of bug spray.

He had missed the post office's opening hours, though, so it would have to wait until tomorrow. Evening had come. He was just considering where he could get another coffee when his phone rang.

Donald Lane. Slim picked up. 'Don?'

'Hey, Slim. Got some information for you. I'm not sure whether this is likely to help you or not, but we'll see.'

'Go for it, Don.'

'Okay, the easy part. That number ... it's not for a phone. My guess is it's some kind of locker pass code or even a number for a combination lock. Could be you're looking for something that needs to be opened.' A pause. 'Right, that was the easy part. The birth certificate ... there isn't one.'

Slim nearly dropped his phone. 'What are you talking about?'

'I've done a national search, even talked to a mate who works in a governmental database department. There are lots of Emilia Martins and even a few Emilia Louise Martins, but only three who would currently be sixteen years old, and none of those has a parent named Georgia or James. And the closest of those to where you are is in Birmingham. I did a bit more background work and found active social media accounts for all three, in case you wanted to check your girl against some pictures.'

'Thanks, Don, but that probably won't be necessary. So what you're saying is that Emily has no identity?'

'No registration. I checked and she does have a passport issued, which means somewhere along the line her birth certificate was faked. What it essentially means is that she wasn't born in a hospital, nor was the state ever notified of her birth. To all intents and purposes, your girl doesn't exist.'

30

It was a long, cold walk home in a rain shower that seemed designed to screw with Slim as much as possible. Or perhaps it was some snotty-nosed god who wanted his jacket washed as per Bernadette's request.

Georgia had saved a portion of casserole for him, but after taking one look at his clothes, she ordered him upstairs to the shower, issuing a withering, 'Why didn't you call? James would have picked you up.' Slim responded by holding up his battery-less phone, although he would have walked anyway. Even with the rain he had wanted time to gather his thoughts before returning.

The casserole tasted bitter as he mulled over what to say to Georgia and James. He wished they had some hateful extended family he could grill for gossip, but it looked increasingly likely that he would need to confront the pair—and in particular Georgia—on certain matters if his investigation were to progress further. And that opened up the possibility of not getting paid, something that would leave him searching for a decent bridge to sleep under.

After dinner, Georgia asked him politely for an update, and he told her something vague about a similar disappearance he had uncovered, a tale he made up on the spot to keep her off his back, told with enough authority to be convincing. It did the trick, but he knew somewhere along the line he would have to come clean.

How much might she have been involved, anyway? Surely the woman—as polite and subservient a person as he had ever met—couldn't also be a cold-hearted monster capable of faking the abduction of her own child?

And if she had, why on earth would she hire him to carry out an investigation?

As always, it seemed best to start with James, looking for cracks in the man's armour. The following morning, when James mentioned a walk into town to pick up some bread, Slim offered to accompany him.

The skies had cleared overnight but it was still chilly as they walked up the hill to the town centre. Slim stuffed his hands into his pockets and said nothing, waiting for James to initiate a conversation to fill the growing awkwardness. In the end the man took the bait, muttering, 'It must be an interesting life, you know, being a private investigator.'

Slim shrugged. 'It has some moments you might call exciting, but a lot of it is drudge work, following up leads that go nowhere, digging up family histories, that kind of thing.'

'Oh? Have you dug up much of ours?'

'I haven't had call to,' Slim said, a little too hastily, covering his back. 'I think it's unlikely anything in your past is relevant, unless you had an enemy you've not told me about.'

James was quiet for a moment. 'Not that I recall ... none that would do such a thing.'

'And it looks like you've had a happy marriage,' Slim continued, trying to lay a trap. 'I mean, you look happy enough together now, despite everything.'

James shrugged. 'We've had our ups and downs. Georgia might come across as lovely, but she was a bit more of a firebrand in her younger days.'

A closed-doors dragon, Lisa May had said.

Slim chuckled. 'I was married once,' he said. 'I know how it goes. My wife used to kick me out at least once a week,' he added, trying to buddy up to James, offer a matey hand to any of James's long-held frustrations. In truth, his wife had rarely been there during their brief time together, fleeing from his drinking into the arms of her various lovers.

'Sounds familiar,' James said, but just as Slim thought the floodgates of repressed emotions would break loose, James looked up at a bakery's window and said, 'Ah, here's the place.'

He looked relieved to go inside. Slim, who had claimed a visit to the library, could do nothing but wave a hand in farewell through the shop window and then head on up the street.

After briefly stopping in at the post office to pick up his package from Alan, Slim bypassed the library, heading straight for Coronation Park and the leisure centre on its lower edge. Halfway up the hill, though, the bruises on his ribs made him pull up, gasping for breath. He wondered if perhaps he had cracked one as he leaned on the open gate leading to a wide, private driveway. Through the trees a camera mounted on the wall of a large two-storey house pointed in his direction, a red light blinking.

Slim hadn't got around to asking Graham Reeves about the footage from the CCTV cameras, but since he

Eight Days

was here and the prospect of a further hill climb was daunting, he decided to check for himself.

He walked up the drive and knocked on the front door.

'I'm afraid we don't accept cold callers,' fluted an old woman's voice through an intercom beside the door. 'Our house is linked to the local police station so I would ask you to leave our property.'

Not in the mood for a conversation with someone so snooty, Slim didn't even bother to introduce himself, and hurried back down the driveway with her warning ringing in his head.

The next house up had a solitary camera which pointed at the front door, but the owner was far friendlier, and told Slim to have a word with "Andy" from two doors farther up.

Andy turned out to be a retired soldier with a paranoid streak after being wounded in the Falklands war. He walked with a limp and was only too pleased to invite Slim in after Slim gave him a brief summary of what he was after.

'Damn pigs couldn't find their big toe if it was wedged up their own backsides,' he said, leading Slim into a narrow kitchen, then immediately going to a cupboard to fetch a bottle and two glasses. Slim balked at the sight of the whisky, but it was too late to back out as Andy handed him a tumbler.

'To the British army,' Andy said, holding up the glass. 'The finest maker of men in the world, and an even greater breaker of them.' He drank, then stood there waiting, his head cocked, eyes watching Slim with expectation like a drill sergeant demanding an attention. Slim opened his mouth to protest, to tell Andy he had been dry for nearly nine months, his longest period since his teenage years, but under the weight of Andy's gaze he felt like a tired fish being drawn into shore after a long battle.

He lifted the glass. The liquid slid down his throat like a deadly snake. It hit his stomach with an outward blooming of heat and comfort, making Slim sigh. As his arms and legs tingled, he found himself taking a seat, looking up as Andy refilled his glass then stumbled across the room to a chair opposite.

'So, what can I help you with?'

It only took a couple of minutes for the booze to lower his guard. Soon the words were pouring out of Slim's mouth as he told this near stranger who he was and what he was doing wandering around outside and that he had no clue which direction the investigation was going to take and that his biggest fear was not that he would never solve it but that the Martins themselves would turn out to be responsible and he wouldn't get paid.

(And and and)

Andy seemed to understand, nodding along sagely, dropping in the odd comment. The pigs couldn't be trusted. The rich were a close network designed to keep themselves there, the government was spying on you, and the only person safe to trust was yourself. Slim's glass was refilled, then again. The investigation began to fade into the background, so that even when Andy began to talk about what Slim had hoped to learn, he could only focus on the bottle.

'And there's that one guy I don't trust. They came for the footage but I made sure to copy it.' Something was being thrust into Slim's hand. 'Of course it never came back, as I thought. And then some pig told me to take down the camera on the gate. Said it infringed on public privacy, whatever the hell that means. The shifty one, that was. The thug. Reeves. Wanted to kick him off my land, the nosy sod. You watch out for him.'

'Uh huh.'

Slim was unsure what part he had taken in the conversation but he became aware of a door approaching him as though it were moving and not him, and a clammy hand was shaking his and wishing him well.

The sunlight outside was too bright. Slim winced as he stumbled up the road, sure there was something else he had planned for the afternoon, but trying with all his might to walk away from where he knew there to be local pubs, where he could upgrade and finish the devastation he had already started. The years of struggle had given him a stubborn resilience against relapsing, one which usually meant he headed for the nearest field, determined to put as much wilderness between himself and further temptation as he could, in the hope that his legs would give out before his willpower did.

He heard laughter as he stumbled through Coronation Park, unsure from where it came although aware he was passing the navy-blue- and black-clad bodies of school kids returning home, some veering off the path to avoid him.

As he came towards a particularly large group of blurred faces, he decided to do the distancing for them, stumbling off the path and continuing on through the freshly mown playing field, his feet kicking up clumps of cut and drying grass and weeds as he ran faster and faster as the field steepened.

Where was Bernadette? He hadn't seen her for several days. Was she all right? Was she avoiding him?

He had always met her somewhere through these trees. He could no longer locate the path, so he pushed through the undergrowth, pushing branches out of his face and handfuls of weeds away from his legs.

Somewhere up here, but he could hardly see anything. There was a bench ... where was it? A gravel path, a pond—

His foot came down but there was nothing beneath it. A duck quacked like a mocking alert on a slapstick comedy show, then reeds brushing his legs slowed his descent just enough that his vision cleared in time to see the water coming up to meet him.

31

'Are you aware that you looked like a complete plonker?'

Bernadette stood somewhere above him. Slim looked down and found dry ground below his legs, although he couldn't immediately recall how he had gotten out of the water. He was soaked from the waist down, bits of pondweed and sand stuck to his jeans.

His head still spun but the cold shock had brought his senses back, and when he looked up to find Bernadette squatting beside him, holding out a gym towel with a school logo on it, he almost saw her clearly. No smile, just a look of disappointment in her eyes.

'Go on, take it. It's not mine, anyway. I got it from the lost property box inside the leisure centre.'

Slim took the towel. His head was thumping, his arms and legs aching as though his very blood hurt.

'I fell off the wagon,' he said.

'I noticed. Right into the pond. Funniest thing I've seen in ages, although I'm not one for laughing all that much.'

Slim reached for her arm and pulled her close. 'If I try

to leave ... if I try to get more booze, stop me. Please.'

'How am I supposed to do that?'

Slim pulled a box out of his coat pocket. The outer packaging was wet, but the object Alan had sent him was safe inside a sealed freezer bag.

'What the hell is this?'

'A police-issue taser. It's fully charged. Point it at me and click.'

'Are you serious?'

'Yes. Don't hesitate. It has a range of three meters. I've put it to the highest setting.'

'Don't these things cause brain damage?'

'I don't know about that, but I don't care. The highest setting. Nothing is more dangerous to me right now than the booze.'

Bernadette stared at him. 'Yes,' she said slowly. 'I get it.'

The disappointment in her eyes was damning. Slim looked away, not wanting her to see his tears.

'You know, I was so mad at you,' Bernadette said. 'You didn't need to mess with Carter. He went straight to my dad. You know what my dad did?'

'No.' Slim closed his eyes, wishing he could close his ears too.

'He wrapped a tea towel round my neck and told me he'd kill me if I went to any of his contacts again. Luckily he was also drunk so he didn't have the strength to do any damage. You people are a mess, aren't you?'

'Us people.' Slim stared at the ground. 'I'm sorry,' he said. 'I didn't think. And about your father ... I'll help you.'

Bernadette gave a bitter laugh. 'Help me? How? Help yourself first.'

'I could ... could ... talk to him.'

Bernadette shrugged. 'Three months and I'm out of

there,' she said. 'First thing on my sixteenth I'll be down the council signing on for a flat. Happy birthday to me.' Then, with a long sigh, she added, 'Come on, get up.'

She helped him over to the bench. His sodden clothes were taking on his body heat, making him feel like he was sitting in a smelly, warm bath.

'Okay, so I think you're a pathetic arsehole, but I'm prepared to forgive you if you sort your shit out,' Bernadette said. 'Did you manage to learn anything from beating up my dad's drug dealer?'

Talking about the case might help to keep his mind off the booze. He went through what he had learned since last talking to Bernadette. The girl listened attentively, then shrugged.

'All a lot of spec, really. You don't have much hard to go on.'

'The birth certificate? If she was never registered at a hospital, that's got to be something, hasn't it?'

'Ask her mum straight out.'

'It won't go down well. I'm supposed to be finding out who abducted Emily at fourteen, not why she doesn't have a birth certificate.'

'It could all be connected.'

'I don't see how.'

Bernadette punched him on the arm. 'Think outside the box, Slim. Come on, you're the detective.'

He tried, but for once the booze was no help, his mind an empty shell, his last thoughts rattling around like pieces of broken glass, too many missing to ever make a whole picture ... but maybe there was something. Something on the edge of his vision which wouldn't quite come into focus.

'I can't....' He shook his head, angry and frustrated. It had never been like this before. If there was one thing the booze had ever done for him, it was to twist his perception, sometimes allow him to look at a case from a perspective he had never considered. Perhaps he had finally fried what part of his intelligence was left, because as he stared at the pond's shimmering water, his mind was blank.

'Nothing makes sense,' he said at last.

'Go back to basics,' Bernadette said. 'Break it down into chunks. You know how I deal with the crap I get at home and at school? I break it into pieces. Get through breakfast. Make it to school, survive until mid-morning break. Survive to lunch, then find somewhere where no one will see me until I can go back to class. I don't even think about the days.'

Slim looked at her, feeling a sudden bloom of sorrow worse than anything he had felt before. He was an older man with all of life's experiences to spur him on, yet this girl with few was coping better than he. And when he should have been helping her, she was helping him.

'Slim, for Christ's sake, snap out of it,' Bernadette said, shoving his arm, and he realised he had been slowly sliding on to his side. 'I watched you on the TV, saw a program about your last case. You're a genius.'

Her words only made him feel worse, but he gritted his teeth, trying to concentrate.

'Take it one piece at a time,' Bernadette said. 'For example, where was she found?'

'On the path near to Polson. Just back from the road.'

'So ask yourself this, why would someone put her there?'

'I don't know.'

'Well, I've been thinking about it, and it seems there are three possibilities.'

'Okay....'

Bernadette lifted a hand and counted on her fingers.

Eight Days

'One, it was random, but that's the least likely. You don't dump a body somewhere random unless it's a spur of the moment thing, and after eight days, it's unlikely that you're still being spontaneous. Second, it's convenient. The abductor might have lived nearby, walked on that path, or the road might've been on their route to work or whatever.'

Slim nodded. 'And the third?'

'It's symbolic of something. Didn't you tell me a canary was found sitting in a tree nearby?'

'That's right.'

'So symbolic seems likely.'

'But symbolic of what?'

Bernadette beamed, her face lit up with the broadest smile, one Slim hadn't thought her capable of making. It shed the weight of struggle like an unwanted skin, and for a moment she wasn't the downtrodden bullied kid with the dysfunctional family, she was a young girl certain she was praiseworthy, proud of what she'd done.

'I looked it up,' she said, 'and I figured it out. I was angry at you for getting me into trouble but I had to come and tell you. That's the exact spot where the girl killed herself.'

'Smelly Sue? Susan Cole-Bridger?'

'Yes. And get this. She was found there on June 20th, right?'

'That's right.'

'Well, no one ever spotted it because she must have lain there overnight. If she was placed there on June 19th, at more or less nine pm, she would have been placed there exactly, almost to the minute, forty years after Susan's death. Now, you tell me that's not a coincidence.'

Slim stared at her. Then, with a wry smile, he shook his head.

'And you call me a genius,' he said.

32

He hadn't liked watching Bernadette leave for home, a growing sense of protectiveness reluctantly allowing her to convince him there was nothing to worry about, that she had survived her train-wreck parents this long and would continue to do so. The girl was stronger and more resilient than any girl of fifteen ought to be, and as he watched her walk away, he felt like a father watching his child leave for war. Long after she was out of sight he lingered in place, debating whether to follow.

In the end, the ongoing dampness of his clothes and a growing weariness caused by the alcohol shocking his system made him head home too. Georgia had left him a slice of pie and some roast potatoes in a casserole dish, but after poking his head around the living room door to say goodnight, he went to bed, sleeping long and heavy.

The next morning he felt like someone had got after him with a piece of two by four, but after a coffee and reheating the food left for him the night before, he felt a little better. He sat at the kitchen table with a second

Eight Days

coffee, staring out at the pre-dawn dark, the lights of the houses across the field just visible.

He wondered if it was worth interviewing the occupants of those properties, canvassing them under the guise of Mike Lewis, perhaps. Emily's room would have been visible from some of their back windows, after all.

He had woken to a couple of missed calls on his phone, the result of sleeping so early. One was from Kay, the other an unknown number. Today was set to be a long day: James planned to take him on a second visit to Graham Reeves, although Slim was doubtful the abrasive policeman would be of much further help. Then in the evening he had another night school class, and for days had been mulling over whether to approach Emily. At the very least he needed to get another look at the car and its driver.

And somewhere in between, he had to return to the site of yesterday's humiliation and retrieve the computer drive given to him by Andy which had fallen out of his pocket when he fell into the pond.

He couldn't take the risk of a further relapse by visiting Andy again, so prayed he could find it. Whatever information it held could be vital. He hadn't even realised it was gone until he got up and checked the pockets of his stinking coat before stuffing the thing into the washing machine, obeying Georgia's request to wash his clothing separate to theirs. The little flash drive now lay somewhere in the muck at the bottom of the pond in Coronation Park, keeping its secrets.

The day was lightening. The washer finished its cycle with a click and a beep, so Slim took his clothing outside onto a back patio and hung it on the Martins' swivel washing line. Light was creeping across the garden, pushing the shadows back. Slim looked up at the house, surprised to see a figure standing at Emily's window, backed by the room light as the dawn sun shone on his face. He was staring out across the field. At first Slim thought he was enjoying the dawn, but after a few seconds of quiet observation Slim realised the man's gaze was tilted, his eyes focused on the gateway across the field to the right. Slim couldn't see it from the patio, but James's vision didn't waver.

And one other thing it took Slim a moment to realise: despite not having heard the shower or any sound of movement from upstairs, James appeared fully clothed, as though he had been up all night.

33

'Slim. I tried to call you last night.'

'I know. Sorry, Kay, I had something going on.'

For privacy, Slim had walked up the road to a churchyard, where he now sat among tilting, lichen-covered graves, looking out at a view across the back of the castle grounds towards Newport.

'I've got the information you were after.'

'Great, go ahead.'

'First, the sand. You're right, there was a match between the two samples. However, one was clearly cut with river sand, the commercial dredged type.'

'Sounds like I've uncovered a fraud case at a builder's merchant,' Slim said with a wry smile. 'One for the local papers.'

'A merchant run by an idiot,' Kay said. 'River sand is cheap as chips. I imagine they're spending more cutting it with their own.'

Slim couldn't guess at the economics of it all, so gave a shrug. 'What else?'

'Still working on the powder. My contact thinks it's

something pharmaceutical, a painkiller of some sort. It's not anything Class A. He was able to rule that out. He's currently running tests to see if it matches anything on the current market.'

'That's brilliant. Thanks, Kay.'

'And the painting ... well, it's a tough one because it was done by a child. I'm not convinced on a couple of letters, but it appears to be a girl's name.'

'Emily?'

'No. Annabel.'

'Annabel?'

Slim shivered as a breeze rippled his spare jacket, much lighter than the one currently drying on the Martins' line.

'You're sure?'

'About ninety-five percent. That's what she intended to write. Do you know someone by that name?'

Slim shook his head. 'No one. That's the problem.'

'I'm sure you'll figure it out. If you need anything else, give me a shout. I'll try to get the results on that powder back by the end of the week.'

'Thanks, Kay.'

'Look after yourself, Slim.'

Slim ended the call and pocketed his phone.

Annabel? Of the dozens of names he had come across during his investigation, it was one he had never seen. Who was she? A sister who had perhaps died young of some illness?

Neither Georgia nor James had ever mentioned another child, but there were a lot of things they had never mentioned. The existence of another child could be one of many.

Slim stared out across the valley, desperate for an answer. All he had was yet more questions. The sand. The medicine stuffed into Emily's mattress. And now another name. A dead person's name.

He pulled out his phone and was thinking of calling Don when he remembered the other call from last night, the number he didn't recognise. He leaned back on the bench and pressed redial.

'Yeah?' came an aggressive voice after a few rings. 'Who is this?'

'It's Slim Hardy,' Slim said.

'Who? What do you want? You know what time it is?'

Slim recognised the voice now, and lifted an eyebrow in surprise. Julian Carter.

'Why did you call me?'

'What are you talking about? Who is this?'

With a sudden realisation, Slim remembered the assumed name Bernadette had given him. 'It's Johnny,' he said.

'Ah, right.'

'So why did you call me?'

'I thought of something,' Carter said. 'So I played your little game. You didn't make it easy, did you?'

Slim had never expected to hear from Carter again, particularly after getting jumped by a couple of the dealer's mates.

'What game?'

'With your number. You asked me to call if I remembered something. Well, I did. Worth two hundred.'

'Depends what it is.'

'A hundred then.'

Slim sighed. He was likely being played for a fool, but if Carter had resisted spending the money long enough to line the notes up by serial number, he might have something useful to say.

'All right.' Slim glanced at his watch. 'I have an hour.

Where can I meet you?'

'Castle grounds.' A snigger. 'By the old dungeons.'

～

The old dungeons were nothing more than grassy pits at the lower end of the castle grounds, surrounded by collapsed stone walls. Slim was reading the National Trust information sign when he saw Carter approaching.

The man was alone, walking in the frantic shuffle-hunch Slim always associated with drug abusers, wearing a hoodie, hands stuffed into pockets, eyes flicking everywhere except at Slim as though afraid of who might be watching.

'You made it,' he said by way of greeting, showing no sign of regret or remorse over what his mates had done to Slim in the alley beside the chip shop on Newport Industrial Estate.

'Yeah, I did.'

'Got the money?'

'Yeah. Tell me what you remembered.'

'Let me see it.'

Slim rolled his eyes and pulled a handful of notes out of his jacket pocket.

Carter's eyes brightened and he gave a crooked smile.

'Well, you know, you kind of caught me by surprise down there, manhandling me like that. Couldn't remember everything, could I?'

'What have you now remembered?'

'I did know her a bit, eh.'

'Who?'

'The girl. Emily.'

'You knew her? So you lied to me?'

'Nah, just forgot to say, didn't I? And we weren't like mates or anything, but I knew her a bit.'

Eight Days

'Explain, please.'

'Met her up the youth club one night. We hung out.'

Slim didn't want to ask in what way; Carter was at least ten years older than Emily. He just waited for Carter to continue.

'Weird girl, not able to speak and all that. Carried a pad of paper in her pocket to write things on.'

'Go on.'

'She told me about her mum's work, said she could get me some stuff.'

'What stuff?'

'Meds. Strong counter stuff. I cut it with street stuff, give it an extra kick. Anyway, I started buying some off her. She'd text me when she'd got some and her parents were out, and I'd meet her down the end of her garden. One day, I'm down there, handing over some cash, and she just freezes. Looks up over my shoulder like she's seen a ghost and just starts whimpering. Like she's scared. I turn me head and there's this car parked up by the gate and this woman is round the back, opening up the boot, getting something out.'

'What did Emily do?'

'She can't talk, see, so she just starts shaking her head, stuffs the gear into my hand, pockets the money and runs inside. I've got to see my woman anyway, so I scarper. Figured it might have been her mother or something, checking up on her.'

'So you didn't see the woman's face?'

'Nah. But it wasn't her mother.'

'You said you didn't see her face—'

'Nah. But her mother was old, like. And this woman, I saw what she was getting out of the boot.'

'What?'

'A pram. A baby's pram.'

34

Slim was lost in his thoughts on the drive over to see Graham Reeves. He went over his last words with Carter again and again, wondering what significance they might hold.

'It was big, not like a newborn's, but one of those heavy duty things. You could have fit a family of four inside.'

Slim had paid up, but only after calling Carter out on the mugging he had endured. One look at the expression of surprise in Carter's face had told him what he had come to believe, that the lowlife dealer had not been involved, and the timing had been coincidental.

Which meant someone else was watching him, planning to take him out.

He needed to watch his back more than ever.

On arrival, they had barely greeted the stern-faced Detective Graham Reeves before James made his excuses and headed out for a walk.

'I'm surprised you haven't given up yet,' Reeves said, unsmiling, as he poured Slim a coffee from a filter jug.

'Most would have. Or is your day rate too good to give up?'

Slim forced a smile as though the man had cracked a joke, but inside he was bristling.

'My investigation is ongoing,' he said. 'I believe there are several lines of enquiry not yet exhausted.'

'Said like a true media spokesman.'

'No cold case is ever really cold, is it?'

Reeves smiled. 'At last, something you and I can agree on. Did you have any specific questions you wanted to ask?'

'I want to know if Emily Martin has ever been in trouble, specifically before the incident took place.'

'The abduction.'

'You can call it as you like.'

'You don't think she was abducted?'

The word had been a slip of the tongue by Slim, but the speed with which Reeves had questioned him raised more hackles of suspicion. And he remembered the canary in the hall.

'I think there are a multitude of possibilities,' he said. 'Abduction is just one of them. Had she ever been in trouble?'

Reeves sighed. 'A couple of times. Nothing was pinned on her directly, but we'd pulled her in a couple of times as part of a group. The usual teenager stuff. Drinking underage, making a nuisance of themselves in the town centre of a weekend. She was never charged with anything, but got a stern warning to buck her ideas up. From myself on one occasion. I told her she was becoming a disappointment to her parents.'

Slim was quiet for a moment. Then he said, 'So you could say that the abduction—or whatever I should call it

—took place at the height of a period of unruly behaviour?'

Reeves frowned. 'Not at all. She was being a teenager. That was all.'

'I heard she failed her end of year exams just a couple of weeks beforehand.'

'Where did you hear that?'

Slim smiled, thinking how happy it would make Bernadette to hear it said. 'From one of my sources.'

'Lucky you. Inconsequential. Those tests are meaningless and most of the kids know it.'

'As an example of changing behaviour, though?'

'Are you suggesting she was abducted as a form of punishment?'

'I'm not suggesting anything. It's a possibility, that's all. I'm just trying to get an idea of her state of mind leading up to the abduction. I want to know if she might have been in a position of heightened vulnerability. Her incapability to cry out for help already left her disadvantaged.'

'I agree. That's why we checked the CCTV cameras along her likely route with great care.'

Slim held off calling Reeves out on the footage Andy had provided, until he had had a chance to recover and hopefully watch it. He said, 'You said you've been a friend of the family for a long time. How long?'

'Since before Emily was born. I was friends with Georgia first, and later James, after they married.'

'Are you married yourself?'

'I was. My wife passed away three years ago. A hereditary heart condition. I was in a hole for a while but now I'm fine.'

Slim offered his condolences, then made a show of taking his coffee to the bay windows and looking out over

Eight Days

the garden. As he turned around, he scanned the room, but not a single framed photograph was anywhere to be seen. It could be suspicious, or it could just be the actions of a man in mourning, he reminded himself.

'It must be hard for you to talk to me, knowing that I haven't discounted the Martins from my line of enquiry,' Slim said.

'You're wasting your time. They're as good a couple of people as you're likely to meet.'

'Nothing would make me happier than to prove it and write them off,' Slim said. 'There are a couple of things, though. James seems to sleep in Emily's room. Are you aware of any marital trouble?' He forced himself not to smile. 'As a family friend?'

'I'm not, but if you had any inkling of sensitivity you might understand how there could be.'

Slim, feeling chastised, nodded. 'Point taken. However, it's hard to shed any suspicion of the Martins when they act so secretive. If they had been straight with me from the start perhaps I would be done by now and off their payroll.'

'Georgia especially is a very proud woman.'

'I've noticed.' He didn't add that in addition he considered her if not blind, then severely blinkered.

'Let's put it this way. If the Martins had been involved in their daughter's abduction, we would have known. They're not exactly hardened criminals.'

'People can always surprise. I've heard that Georgia was at home on the day of the abduction. Where was James? Your police report says only that he had a clear alibi.'

Reeves sighed. 'He was with another woman.'

Slim nodded. 'And she lives in Newport, doesn't she?'

'How do you know?'

'Because I saw him up there, when he has no need to be.'

Reeves rubbed the bridge of his nose. 'Then you have your answer about why he was sleeping in Emily's room. I believe you're sleeping in their other spare room, are you not?'

'Yes. Who is she?'

'I don't know. It's no business of mine.'

'Why doesn't Georgia throw him out?'

'I told you. She is all about appearances. And he has money. He got sent down, but he had other investments that his lawyers kept out of the investigation. He's a well-off man, which is how he's kept Georgia as a housewife for years, since shortly after Emily was born. I don't like to tell you this, because it's personal and private and I believe has no bearing on the investigation. She suffered terrible post-natal depression and had to give up her job. She's likely still on medication, particularly after all this stress with Emily these last couple of years. It's one reason why I believe you should give up this ridiculous witch hunt and stop sponging the Martins' money. Georgia is a sick lady, not in her right mind.'

Slim decided not to mention that he was yet to see a penny of the Martins' money. With this new information, he needed to get Don back on the case, but Reeves seemed in a sharing state of mind.

'What was her job? Before she gave it up? I heard she was a nursery school teacher.'

'Oh, that was years ago,' Reeves said. 'She gave that up due to stress long before she even met James, from what she's told me. No, at the time when Emily was born, she was working as a pharmacist.'

35

He found Bernadette sitting beside the pond, a can of Coke and a half-eaten Mars bar beside her as she dredged through the weeds with a net.

'How did you know?' Slim said, as she raised a hand to wave.

'Dumbass,' she said, giving him a smile. 'I saw you fall in, remember? And I saw something fall out of your pocket. You were so deep in drama yesterday that I forgot about it, but when I got home I remembered. I came up here early before school but I've not found it yet.' She held up a plastic container filled with rusty items. 'So far I've found one pound forty in change, an old dog collar, and a set of car keys. I'll hand them into the leisure centre later, but they're so rusted they probably belong in a museum by now.'

Slim smiled. 'No flash drives?'

Bernadette shook her head. 'Not yet, but I wouldn't worry. Those things are indestructible. Washed one with maths coursework on it three times and it still worked. Had to soak it in bleach before it gave up. Worst-case scenario is yours got eaten by a duck.'

'I don't see any dead ducks.'

'Then we keep looking.' She handed him the net. 'And I'm tired so it's your turn.'

As Slim dipped the net into the water, he said, 'I don't know how I can thank you for helping me.'

Bernadette shrugged. 'You could write me a reference for police college.'

'What? You want to join the police?'

Bernadette shrugged. 'Why not? If all you do is figure out cases like this all day, it could be interesting.'

Slim smiled. 'I'd love to do it. I'm not sure that a homeless, alcoholic ex-convict is quite the reference you need.'

'Skip all that part and go straight to the celebrity detective part.'

Slim winced. 'I was on TV once. And it wasn't a pleasant experience.'

'Once more than me. How about we wait until you've solved this case then?'

'I appreciate that you have so much faith in me, but I'm not sure it can be solved. Too many people are hiding secrets.'

'Then don't we need to kick the wasps' nest?'

Slim smiled. 'That's one way to look at it.'

He dropped the net into the water, and this time it snagged on something. With a tug, it came free with a USB drive tangled in a thread of pondweed.

'Nice one,' Bernadette said, patting him on the arm. Then, with a matronly scowl, she added, 'Don't lose it again.'

The bus to Tavistock was almost empty. Slim still felt queasy from yesterday's relapse as it bumped along the country lanes.

He had left the flash drive on a windowsill to dry out, but whatever it might show, he had other things to worry about. The lady with the pram. The medicine Emily was selling to Carter. The sand. The damn sand.

He now had a motive for the abduction, if the link was anything more than simple coincidence. Someone wanting Susan Cole-Bridger remembered. But who? And why Emily?

He reached the community centre and slipped into his seat just as the class got underway. As before, he made a show of writing down the teacher's words while keeping an eye on the girl sitting a few rows in front of him, his mind reeling as he tried to create a reason why he, a man of nearly fifty, would have need to strike up a conversation with a sixteen-year-old girl.

In the break between classes, he found himself standing by the coffee machine. Emily was sitting alone near the window, staring out through the glass. A couple of other students had bought drinks and were going over their notes. Slim noticed Emily's hands were empty, and happened on to an idea. He pressed a button on the machine, then muttered, 'Ah,' with a dramatic sigh, watching the machine pour hot chocolate into a paper cup. With a frustrated shake of his head, he lifted the cup, frowned, and looked around. Emily wasn't watching, so he walked over and cleared his throat.

'Excuse me,' he said. 'I made a mistake with the machine. I wanted coffee but I got hot chocolate instead. Would you like it? I can't handle all the sugar.' With a smile, he added, 'It keeps me up all night.'

The girl turned, and for the first time Emily Martin looked into Slim's eyes. Up close she had more of James in her than Georgia, soft around the jaw, cheeks slightly rosy, eyebrows heavy over pale blue eyes.

'Thank you,' she said.

36

He awoke with a feeling that he had missed an opportunity. Too stunned to respond after Emily Martin had spoken, he had watched her drift back to class, then later disappear out into the dark before he could follow. By the time he had made it outside to the car park, she had gone.

Everyone told him she was vocally impaired. But she had spoken to him without any kind of inflection in her voice, as though she had no trouble speaking at all. He hadn't heard her speak again for the rest of the class, but that meant nothing. Someone was lying to him, and he felt like a fly caught in a spider's trap.

Georgia had come in while he was out and had tidied his room, folding his clothes, setting his shoes neatly. He had wanted to holler at the sight of it, scream into the woman's face that he was sick of her lies and secrets, that he needed to know the truth or he was done.

But both she and James had gone out. He drank a strong coffee, and his anger faded.

He walked up into town and called Don from a bench outside the church.

'Don, it's Slim. I need you to check a couple of things for me.'

'Sure. How's the case going?'

'Been better. I have a name, and an association with death. Annabel. I need to know if she's a real person. Most likely she died young, in infancy perhaps. And I'd say the southwest is your catchment area.'

'Good God, Slim, you don't ask for much. Do you have a surname or estimated date of death?'

'No surname. But I would guess the death would have been around ten years ago. Sorry I can't be more specific.'

'All right, that's better than nothing. I'll see what I can do.'

'Thanks. One other thing.'

Don chuckled. 'Okay. But make it a little easier, could you?'

'I need more information on Georgia Martin. I heard she used to be a pharmacist. I need to know when and where.'

'Okay. I can pull some tax and national insurance records. That should be easy.'

～

Slim headed back to the house. The Martins had returned from a trip to Tesco. Slim asked James for a lift over to Newport under the pretence of meeting Dave Brockhill again. James agreed, and half an hour later they were driving across town.

They drove into Dave Brockhill's estate and Slim asked James to pull into a cul-de-sac to let him out.

'I'll be an hour,' he said, closing the door. He lifted a

hand to wave, then turned and ducked into an alleyway. Breaking into a sprint, he ran up a slope behind a row of houses and emerged on a grass verge bordering the main road past the estate. He had scoped out the alleys during his previous visits, and knew James had to pass this way to go back into town. Unless he could reverse and turn the car with professional speed, James couldn't have reached the main road before Slim. While it was possible he had chosen to visit a garden centre a couple of miles up the road, having been to the supermarket this morning, Slim found it unlikely.

After waiting half an hour just in case, Slim walked back around the estate until he located James's car innocuously parked along the curb between two others. Slim did another circuit, checking which houses had cars outside, where people were likely to be at home, then found an alleyway with the best view of the street. Glancing at his watch, he saw his hour was almost up. A door opened and closed farther up the street. James stepped out, said goodbye to a woman of whom Slim caught the briefest of glimpses, and then walked down to the street, hands in pockets. Slim ducked out of sight then headed down the alley, skirting around until he reached the place where James had dropped him off.

A moment later, James's car appeared and pulled into the curb.

'Productive morning?' James asked.

'Very,' Slim said as he climbed in.

~

Slim walked back into town after lunch alone. He had planned to go back over to Newport but to his disappointment he had missed the last bus, so decided to give the arduous hike through the valley a miss. Instead, he headed for the library. There he went back online, this time browsing through the blogs of both St James's College and the local primary schools, looking for anything he might have missed. Nothing stood out, so he found an archive room where old local newspapers were stored in huge A2-sized files. The librarian showed him how to look at them, so for a while he flicked through the ancient pages, concentrating on the section near the back of each which highlighted local sports news and school events.

Emily had played volleyball for a local team, and there, a couple of months before her disappearance, was a team photo. Dave Brockhill stood off to one side, a proud look on his face, while a trophy sat between the two girls in the middle. Emily stood on the other side, wearing a substitute's bib, her face impassive.

Slim continued flicking through the pages until his eyes started to ache. He found Emily again in a different section, a few years younger, part of a group putting on a primary school play. The black and white photo wasn't captioned and Slim nearly missed her, but it was certainly her as she stood to the side, dressed as a doctor.

Figuring she was getting too young to recognise, he began to flick forward again, looking for anything he had missed. Shortly before he gave up, he found her once more, on an adjacent page, this time as a member of a local art club. Standing with five others and the teacher, labelled as Mrs. Miller, standing behind them with a hand on Emily's shoulder, the caption below read "highly commended for Launceston Youth Art Club at the Royal Cornwall Show", although the pictures being held up by the kids had lost all detail in the paper's printing. Perhaps that was a forethought causing the kids' glum expressions. Something was odd about the picture but Slim couldn't be sure what. He took a photo of it with his digital camera and decided to hunt out the club.

It would be interesting to know what Emily had painted.

He was just packing up when his phone rang. He waited until he was outside then called Don back.

'Slim, it's me,' Don said. 'This girl Annabel. I think I've found her.'

37

His throat felt dry, his temples throbbed. He sat on a bench at the top of Coronation Park, his hands shaking as he looked at the phone in his hands. Don had hung up, gone to continue his trawl for information, leaving Slim with the bombshell that a girl called Annabel had in fact lived and died within the period he had specified, and that she had, in fact, lived as close as Tavistock.

Annabel Yates, born on September 14th, 2004, had died, aged just seven, on January 7th, 2011. She was buried in a cemetery in Tavistock which Slim had been walking past to visit the community centre for the last two weeks.

There was too much coincidence. Annabel Yates was somehow linked to Emily Martin. And Emily had known it. She had painted the picture of the woman with the pram, and even the grave.

Mummy, Daddy, Annabel.

Why had Emily painted a picture of Annabel's family's graves?

Eight Days

Slim put his head in his hands, squeezing his temples. This was supposed to have been a straightforward case to gently bring him back into the game. If he had any hope of solving it, he had to confront the family of a dead child in a search for answers. The thought of doing so was almost too much to bear.

'Don't do it,' said a familiar voice.

Slim looked up. Bernadette stood in front of him, a bag over her shoulder.

'Don't do what?'

'Drink. Whatever's happened, don't.'

'I wasn't planning to.'

'Yes, you were. I can tell.'

'No, I....' Slim shrugged. 'Maybe I was. I don't know.'

'What happened?'

'Sit down.'

A few minutes later, Bernadette whistled through her teeth. 'That's something, isn't it? Are you going to visit the family?'

'I have to.'

'Any ideas?'

Slim grimaced. 'I've already found them,' he said. 'I finally figured something out.'

'What?'

He pulled a strip of paper out of his pocket and handed it over. 'This is the number I found on the back of the cupboard in Emily's room,' he said. 'It was erased so I had to read it from the depressions in the wood. My friend was wrong about being some kind of serial number. I thought it was a telephone number at first, but when you realise that this six is actually a G, and this eight a B, it becomes a car registration number. I looked online. It belongs to a Ford Escort registered to a Sarah Yates of 14 Yelland Road, Tavistock.'

'So Emily knew who was watching her?'

'It looks that way. She must have recognised the car at some point and written down the registration. I don't know if she ever used it to identify the people watching her, but she clearly knew they were there.'

'And why would they have been watching her?'

'That's what I need to find out. My guess is that the woman who Julian Carter saw was Sarah Yates, and the pram would have been for Annabel.'

'But Annabel's been dead for nine years. Carter said he saw her shortly before Emily's disappearance.'

'If that was the case, what was in the pram?'

'Perhaps I'll ask Sarah Yates when I visit.'

'You can do this, Slim.'

'I can see myself ruining someone's life. Too many questions ... not everyone wants to face the answers.'

'Do you want me to come?'

Slim looked up, and briefly the schoolgirl melted away into someone mature beyond her years. Then the look of the young girl returned, a desperation to help in her eyes.

'I think I'll take that one alone,' Slim said. 'But there are other things you can help me with.'

Together they headed down the hill to the library. On the way, Slim asked Bernadette about the Launceston art club he had seen mentioned in the newspaper.

Bernadette shrugged. 'Yeah, it was in the old youth centre on Tower Street but it closed down a couple of years ago. I never went—obviously—but a few kids used to hang out there. There's a new one up on Pennygillam Industrial Estate now, but I don't know if they have an art club or not.'

'You know who used to run it?'

'How would I know if I never went? More than my

life's worth trying to hang out with the pricks that went down there.'

'I just wondered.'

'Yeah, well, my guess is you never had it hard at school.'

Slim smiled. 'I didn't properly screw up my life until after I quit. My advice would be to not do what I did.'

'Thanks. You're a better role model than my dad, at any rate.'

'I'm guessing the bar is set pretty low.'

'If I had a spade I'd dig a trench,' Bernadette said.

'Are you sure you don't want me to have a word?'

Bernadette gave him a suspicious smile. 'It's all sorted,' she said. Then, at Slim's look, she added, 'Don't worry, he's still alive. I just warned him, that's all.' She patted her pocket. 'Can I keep the taser you gave me?'

'You didn't....'

Bernadette shrugged. 'Just once. You did say to use it to protect myself.'

'Keep the setting low or you'll cause lasting nerve damage.'

'I set it on high.' Bernadette smiled. 'But I'll turn it down from now on.'

They went into the library and found a computer booth in a corner. Squeezing two seats into the small cubby hole, Slim pulled the USB out of his pocket and slid it into a port.

'I'm hoping it's dried out,' he said.

'I told you, they're indestructible,' Bernadette said as an icon appeared on the screen.

Slim opened up the video feed. It was several hours of footage from the day of Emily's abduction. The camera view was from the left-hand gatepost of Andy's place and looked up the street towards the top of Coronation Park.

Slim wound it forward to within an hour of the estimated time of abduction, parked cars appearing and disappearing seemingly by magic. Slim set the time to midday and let the tape run.

'There,' Bernadette said. 'The transit van.'

A white van was indeed parked a little way up the street, its number plate too grainy to read. As Slim watched, it started up the hill, slowing before it reached the top as a small blue car came into view. The car pulled in, allowing the van to move past. The car, visible out of the distant hedge as little more than a blue blob, was still for about a minute before executing a U-turn and heading back in the direction from which it had come. A few seconds later, the white transit reappeared, making its way slowly down the hill, past the parked cars, and passing from view behind the camera.

Bernadette was talking beside him in hushed tones, saying something about computer imaging programs, but Slim shook his head.

'No.' He pointed to a car on the screen. 'This is why the video was hidden. That's Detective Reeves's private car. I saw it parked outside his house.'

The Mercedes sat in the shadows beneath the trees, its tinted windows revealing nothing. The van had been parked behind it, hiding it from the camera's view, but now, revealed, its number plate was clearly legible.

'As in the head of the local police?' Bernadette whispered. 'I remember him coming to school once to do a talk on shoplifting. Pompous dickhead. What's he doing there? Did he take Emily?'

'We're about to find out,' Slim said.

He sped up the video. A couple of cars came and went, including the white van again. Slim suspected it was a local delivery driver, but could see how it had attracted suspicion. The Mercedes didn't move. Then, at around half past one, the driver's door opened, and a person climbed out.

Bernadette clamped a hand over her mouth. 'Oh my God, is that Emily?'

Slim shook his head. 'It's Georgia,' he said.

38

Slim couldn't prove whether either Detective Reeves or Georgia was involved in Emily's disappearance, but the evidence of a suspected affair would throw serious muck at Reeves's career, while the suppression of evidence could result in its end. No wonder Reeves had been so abrasive, and it made Carter's incredulity at being accused of masterminding Slim's mugging all the more believable. Certainly a police chief with a network of contacts and informants had the resources to cause Slim serious headaches. He would do well to keep looking over his shoulder.

Bernadette wanted to know what he would do with this new information, but Slim didn't know. It was something to be banked for the time being, until he could find a use for it later in the investigation.

One thing it hadn't shown, of course, was the identity of Emily's abductor, and Slim reminded himself that he needed to stay on-topic, particularly if he wanted to get paid. Having an affair with a police chief was worth a wrist slap; it wasn't in the same league as a kidnapping.

Eight Days

It would make good leverage with Reeves if necessary, although after being jumped on Newport Industrial Estate Slim was keen to avoid revealing Andy as his source. It might be better to compile more conclusive evidence of Reeves's suppression of evidence and then reveal it anonymously.

When he got back to the house, the Martins had gone out. Slim wasted no time, slipping on a pair of gloves he had bought in a hardware store on the way home and sneaking into the kitchen. He began to check through the drawers one by one, careful not to move anything, aware that his trained eyes would know what he was after when he saw it.

However, he found nothing. Batteries, old shopping receipts, a roll of tape practically melted off its cardboard inner, but nothing that suggested the Martins had secrets to hide. He moved out into a utility room, checking through cupboards and drawers.

Nothing.

Frustrated, he went upstairs, gently opening the Martins' bedroom door to reveal a tidy room with a neatly made bed slightly depressed on one side as though used regularly by only one person. Slim checked Georgia's bedside table and looked in the cupboard underneath, finding only a pile of romance paperbacks and an unopened gift box of facial scrubs.

Next, he went into Emily's room. He had already checked in here, so didn't expect to find anything, but as he pulled open what had been an empty clothes drawer he was presented with a full array of medicines, everything from simple creams and ointments to complex prescription medication. Perhaps they had brought them in here to sort through them, maybe to see what they had left. Or maybe they had feared Slim finding them elsewhere. As he lifted one bottle up and turned it over, he realised had encountered some of these before. One was a strong sedative, another a powerful anti-depression drug. Georgia's name was on the back of one packet, but what was more of a surprise was to find James's name on another.

Other unmarked pills filled clear plastic bags at the back of the drawer. Slim opened one and slipped a pill into his pocket, planning to send it to Kay for analysis.

He was leaning over to close the drawer when the door creaked behind him.

'What on earth are you doing?' James said.

39

Slim, speechless, stared at James. He hadn't heard the man come in nor climb the stairs, but as Slim stood there, James's gaze shifted, eyes scanning the inside of Emily's room.

'It's almost a relief that she's gone,' James said wistfully, the slur in his voice betraying that he had already self-medicated. 'It was always so hard to maintain the charade.'

'What charade? What are you talking about?'

'I mean, when she was young it was all right, because she needed us, but once she hit her teens ... she was locked in a cage and we couldn't hear her. Just this constant ... rage. I never wanted children, you know. I felt I was too old to start, and so it proved. We never connected, Emily and me. It was all for Georgia. Always for Georgia. Always to make her happy.'

'I was looking for photograph albums,' Slim said, finding his voice at last. He held up his hands and smiled. 'Hence the gloves.'

James's face brightened, but his eyes remained glazed. 'Why didn't you just ask?' he said.

Downstairs, Slim made the coffee while James pulled out a couple of boxes from under a shelf and hauled them on to the dining room table. Georgia had previously shown him selected cuts from the same boxes, but James looked in the mood to go through the family history. Slim drank coffee and listened as James went way back, grainy, black and white pictures of grandparents, cousins, relations, talking Slim through family empires and failures, war heroes, domestic nobodies, he who emigrated, she who died young. Slim's interest perked as they moved into the modern era, pictures of James and Georgia at school, class photos. Slim was surprised to discover they had been secondary school classmates—standing on opposite ends of the same row —'but we barely shared a word in three years'—and that Georgia, far from the homely housewife cresting the wave of middle-age, had been something of a looker, regarding the camera with a tilted face and sultry eyes. James, on the other hand, was anonymous, a face easy to pass over, not even looking at the camera in several pictures, strands of untended teenage hair flapping across his face like curtains shutting out the anonymity of the night.

After what felt like an age of James justifying the authenticity of his existence through matey shots of holidays in the Med, and finally wedding photos of a couple in their forties, barely recognisable from their school days, they came on to Emily.

Slim was surprised not to see pictures of a hospitalised newborn, but suspected Emily had been born at home. It was uncommon these days but still happened. Why she had never been registered was a question he still held back. In the first few pictures, of a bedraggled mother holding a tiny thing barely visible among the layers of wrapping,

Eight Days

Georgia looked radiant. Her smile seemed to transcend the picture like a living thing of its own, hypnotic, a sign of pure joy. As the child aged, however, Georgia's happiness faded. James maintained the same reluctant camera smile throughout, and a growing Emily randomly selected from wide, gappy smiles to sullen refusals to look up. Georgia showed a gradual decline, until by Emily's teenage years she was barely standing straight. Slim was desperate to ask about medication and depression but James continued the same dull monotone throughout as though oblivious to the changes in his family.

In the last picture of them together before the abduction, James was a lumbering, aged caricature of himself as a teenager, while Georgia glared angrily at the camera. Emily, gangly and dressed in art project clothes, looked unhappily at the ground.

They gave the impression of a fracturing family. Not uncommon, perhaps, in a family with a troublesome teen and struggling parents, but they would never have a chance to recover. Just a month later, Emily had been abducted, and their whole world had changed.

'Thanks for showing me these,' Slim said, draining the dregs of his third coffee and standing up. 'I really appreciate it. I just need to slip out for a while and run a quick errand.'

James looked up. His eyes held a mixture of hope and worry.

'You know, you can walk away from this anytime,' he said. 'I don't think you'll find the answer, no matter what Georgia says. I think, sometimes, that it's better to just accept the way things are.'

40

Slim's feet felt leaden as he walked through Tavistock town centre. Clouds had rolled in to add a chill to the air and dapple the world with grey, as though somehow reactionary to his mood. He tried to feel emotion as he walked past bakeries and coffee shops, through a small square where a band was playing sixties folk songs to a smattering of applause, past a park where a handful of children chased each other across a concrete courtyard scattered with swings and slides.

It was easier to blank everything out, to turn himself into the stone-hearted purveyor of doom, the plague doctor, the bringer of bad news, the giant with its foot poised to crush the life out of the gummy chick struggling from its egg. Nothing good was coming, and he knew it. He passed the lights of a pub, and knew one for courage would make it easier, but not better.

He walked on.

It had taken a few minutes of searching, but he had found her. In the leafy yard of Tavistock Parish Church, a short walk from the peaceful, tree-lined River Tavy, she had rested in a small, polite grave perhaps reminiscent of her stature in life. *Annabel Kelly Yates. Sept 2004 - Jan 2011. We miss you, love Mum, Dad, and Elizabeth.*

The grave was well-tended, fresh flowers in the pot. A child gone but not forgotten.

He turned onto her street, pausing for a few minutes at the door of a corner pub, its confines hidden behind a heavy door, drapes over the windows. His last chance to back out, his last chance to ride the downward spiral and avoid what was coming next.

He walked on.

Up the street, stopping at a narrow but not unpleasant terrace, a small yard at the front containing a couple of bicycles chained to a fence post, a few flower pots, a stone dog with a sign around its neck which said WELCOME.

Slim resisted the urge to kick it over, or at least face it the other way, as he lifted a hand to ring the bell.

Through the door he heard the muffled sound of the bell echoing through a hall. Clumps like feet on stairs. A girl's voice, calling for her mother.

The door swung open, a girl stepping out of an unlit entranceway to look up at him.

'Yes?' A frown. 'Don't I....'

'Emily Martin?' Slim said, his eyes filling with tears.

41

'You'd be proud of me,' Slim said to Bernadette's silhouette as it stood a few feet away in the dark, feeling absurdly like their roles were reversed. 'I didn't drink. I wanted to, but I didn't.'

'I want to say you're pathetic, but that's just because I'm angry that you got me out of bed. They'd only just stopped shouting long enough for me to sleep. How did you find me?'

Slim let out a laugh that sounded crazy even to him. 'I'm a private detective. It's my job.'

'Really?'

'I looked in the phone book,' Slim said, letting out the same hysterical laugh.

'I think you need to see a psychiatrist,' Bernadette said. 'Something's not right with your head. You should take a holiday.'

'This is supposed to be it.'

Bernadette lit a cigarette. Slim wanted to tell her that at fifteen it was a bad habit, that she should quit before she screwed up her life like he had done with his, but all he could do was flop down on the park bench in the little grove of trees down the road from her house and let out a deflating sigh.

'So don't keep me hanging on,' Bernadette said, standing over him like an interrogation room detective. 'What happened? What did the woman say?'

∽

The woman was crying, trying to close the door, but Slim acted fast, pushing his foot into the space, muscling his way inside. The girl pulled a phone out of her pocket but Slim grabbed her wrist, knocking it away, kicking it behind him and standing over it, keeping a hand on the girl as he fended off the mother's attempts to pull her free. Something died inside him as he strong-armed the gaunt, frail woman and her daughter, pinning them both against the wall before he could finally get a word out over their screams.

'I'm not going to hurt you!' he shouted. 'I just want to talk, then I'll leave. I promise.'

The girl relaxed, but as Slim loosened his grip she aimed a kick at his groin. His military training took over, Slim turning sideways to avoid the blow, bringing up a hand and slamming her back against the wall.

'I won't hurt you!' he said again, holding onto the girl, waiting for the fight to fade out of her. The woman, crying, batted weakly at his arm and he knew she was done. He let her go, watching her slide to the floor, hands covering her face. The girl struggled a few seconds longer until Slim felt her too relax. He twisted her around and released her, watching her drop to the floor to comfort her distraught mother.

'What are you going to do to us?' the woman said.

'Nothing. Absolutely nothing. I just want to talk. I want to talk about Annabel and Emily Martin.'

~

'So you basically broke into a strange woman's house and assaulted her and her daughter,' Bernadette said. 'Jesus, Slim, you're perhaps not the best for a reference after all.'

'I had no choice,' he said, wondering if that were really true or not.

~

A door through to another room was closed. Slim blocked the front door and the stairs. Certain he could catch them if either tried to escape, he lowered himself down.

'I just want to talk,' he said. 'Nothing more. I have questions and I want answers, but I won't hurt you. And then I'll leave.'

'Are you ... are you stalking me?' the girl stammered, provoking a gasp from the woman.

Slim frowned. 'I'd be lying if I said no, but I mean you no harm. I'm looking for Emily Martin. You're her, aren't you?'

'My name is Elizabeth Yates,' the girl said. 'I'm not Emily Martin, but ... I was.' She sniffed. 'For a while.'

The woman started sobbing again. Slim wanted nothing more than to put his fingers in his ears, blocking out everything.

42

'She was or she wasn't?' Bernadette said. 'You'd better get to the point or I'm going back to bed.'

Slim wanted to appreciate her attempt to humour him, but inside he felt dry, like a desert riverbed. He forced a laugh, hoping that in the dark the sadness was hidden from his face.

～

Sarah Yates, the woman, was too frail even to sit without her daughter's help. With some trouble but in the hope they would relax a little, Slim allowed them to go into an adjacent living room where they sat side by side on a two-seater sofa. Slim pulled a threadbare armchair around to face them, leaning forward on the edge in case either made a run for the door.

Taking a few seconds to look around, he established quickly that there was no man to expect home; the larger photographs showed a mother and daughter pairing, the daughter growing taller and stronger as the woman softened and grew frail. Here, too, were signs of the elusive Annabel, a couple of photos tucked behind others that included a frail girl leaning on crutches, her face twisted slightly to the side, her nose a little off centre, her mouth crooked. Questions burned on Slim's tongue, but part of him wished he had never come.

'I'm a private investigator,' he said. 'I was hired to investigate the abduction of Emily Martin.'

'Who hired you?' Sarah Yates asked. Now that he saw her up close, he realised the resemblance to Georgia was coincidental. She wore her hair the same way, was of a similar age. But where Georgia, despite the reliance on medication Slim had uncovered, was robust and full of life, Sarah Yates had the look of an addict or someone long-term sick. She was either dying of something, or had given herself up to the likelihood a long time ago.

'I'd rather not say. Not right now. I want answers to my questions to conclude my investigation, but I need you to know that I don't have to involve the police. What you tell me doesn't have to leave this room.'

Sarah Yates wiped her eyes. 'What do you want to know?'

'Everything.'

'Emily was Elizabeth's sister,' Sarah said, as Elizabeth took her mother's hand and held it tight. 'I never wanted anything bad to happen to her.'

'It might be best to start at the beginning,' Slim said.

Sarah let out a long sigh that Slim feared would turn into more sobbing. With another deep breath she managed to pull herself together.

'I started working at James Martin's firm in 2002,' she said. 'I worked as a secretary. He was a good boss, and a kind man. I liked him a lot.' Her eyes glazed as she revisited the memories. 'I didn't mean for anything to happen between us. It just did.'

Slim lowered his face and closed his eyes. He was aware of Sarah rambling about how she had begun staying late, how James had claimed his marriage was on the rocks, how he had taken pity on her for an ongoing medical condition. He had promised to leave his wife, blah blah; Slim had heard it all before.

'And I found I was pregnant. With twins. Doctors had told me I could never have children. It was a miracle. I'd never been so happy. And then James told me that Georgia was pregnant too.'

Slim looked up. The girl Elizabeth still clutched her mother's hand, but looked uncomfortable, like she wanted to be somewhere else. A boiling rage was growing under Slim's skin, the object of it the seemingly docile man who spent his days pottering in his garden. From Sarah's expression Slim sensed things were about to get worse, and he wondered how he could go home and face James without giving in to the urge to assault the man and punch and punch until nothing recognisable remained.

'It was a difficult birth,' Sarah said, slipping an arm around Elizabeth as though to remind herself of what she had gained. 'I was heavily sedated, and my babies were taken away. I worried for them, feared for their lives. For several days I was medicated, unable to even look at them.' She smiled. 'I named them Elizabeth and Annabel.'

Slim felt a tear beading in the corner of his eye. The worst—the terrible, terrible worst—was yet to come.

'Eventually I got to take my babies home. My beautiful, wonderful twins. However, I was aware early on that Annabel had problems. She didn't look like Elizabeth, and as they grew older, she didn't learn and develop like her. Of course I blamed myself, but Elizabeth was so full of life ... doctors told me Annabel had a rare heart condition. She likely wouldn't reach her tenth birthday. I was heartbroken, of course ... and then one day, we were at the summer carnival, down in the park by the river. And I saw *her*.' Sarah put a hand over her mouth as the tears started to flow again, and it was some seconds before she sobbed, 'And I knew.'

Slim waited. He sensed what was coming. From Elizabeth's expression it was a story she was familiar with, but it might make it easier for her mother if the girl wasn't present.

'Why don't you make your mum a cup of tea?' Slim suggested. Elizabeth frowned at him, but Sarah patted her knee and nodded. The girl lifted an eyebrow which suggested a covert dash for help, but this time Sarah shook her head. 'I believe him,' she whispered. 'He won't hurt us.'

When Elizabeth had gone out, Sarah said, 'I saw them —James and Georgia—with a little girl. She was the image of Elizabeth, and I knew what that witch had done. She had swapped her baby for mine.'

Slim said nothing for a long time. He had a million questions, but his mouth was dry, his heart empty of the cold drive he needed to see this through. He wanted to get up and leave, close the door on the way out and walk away from Tavistock and Launceston and the Martins and never look back.

'I knew what they had done, and I confronted him about it. He would still show up from time to time, pretend to be a dad for a few hours, then vanish back to his perfect family. I told him I knew the children had been swapped. I threatened to go to the police, but he called my bluff. Handed me the phone. I couldn't do it. By then the girls were five, and Annabel, my beautiful broken angel, was getting sicker. Every day I gave that girl all the love I could, and if I made that call ... they'd take her away.'

'It was too late to swap the children back,' Slim said.

Sarah nodded. 'But I still wanted to see my other little girl. So I drove out there often, just to have a look. I left Elizabeth sitting in the car, but I couldn't leave Annabel alone, so I took her in the pram, out into the field behind their house. Just to get a look at her.'

'She saw you,' Slim said.

'I never meant to scare her,' Sarah said, covering her hands with her mouth as the sobs returned. 'If I could have taken all three girls, I would have.'

'And this carried on until Annabel passed away?'

'Yes. And then I told him I wanted my other daughter back.'

'Of course he said no?'

Sarah gritted her teeth. 'He was always devoted to that horrible monster,' she said. 'He would do whatever she wanted and to hell with anyone else. I'd have treated him right. I told him to leave Georgia and bring Emily with him. I knew by then from James that Emily also had a problem—with her speech—and that she was never going to be good enough for wonderful, perfect Georgia. He would have been happy with me, but he refused.'

'So you went to the police?'

'I threatened it again. But he had one over me. He always did. The money.'

'What money?'

The door opened and Elizabeth returned. She handed a mug of coffee to Sarah and sat down beside her. Slim wasn't surprised she hadn't made one for him.

Sarah took Elizabeth's hand with her free hand and squeezed it tight.

'The money I stole from him.'

43

'James did time, didn't he?' Bernadette said, as a car raced past the park, brakes squealing as it made an extravagant turn before powering away down the hill.

Slim nodded. 'He did a few months for embezzlement,' Slim said. 'Money laundering.'

'And Sarah Yates claimed he took the fall for her?'

Slim nodded.

~

'I was desperate,' Sarah said. 'I thought he was going to throw me out on the streets, so I fiddled some books, sent some money overseas. It got spotted almost immediately. James took the fall for me. He was able to hire a good lawyer, get off with little more than a slapped wrist, a few months in a prison no worse than a holiday camp. And he got early release too after it came out that Georgia was pregnant. He got out a few days after the birth.'

'And no one ever found out it was you?'

Eight Days

Sarah gave a sullen shake of the head. 'No. But James said I was looking at five years if the truth came out.'

'And so you stayed quiet?'

'And ... and ... he paid me off.'

'Mum can't work,' Elizabeth said, speaking up for the first time. 'She's on disability for her hip.'

'He promised me ... us ... a better life. All we had to do was play along. He set us up a monthly stipend, and we got on with things. And then Emily disappeared.'

Slim rubbed his eyes. He had hoped for closure, but all he saw now were more doors opening out of this mess.

'She had been gone for eight days when James showed up at the door wanting to speak to Elizabeth.'

'I'd just got back from the beach,' Elizabeth said. 'I was collecting things for an art project. He didn't even let me take a shower.'

Sarah squeezed Elizabeth's hand even tighter. 'He came and took my other baby.'

Elizabeth sighed. 'Only for a while. Until things died down. Then he let me see Mum. Pretended we were going to club events and out for walks.'

Slim shifted on the chair. 'So, let me get this straight. You impersonated your own sister?'

'He put fifty grand into a trust for me,' Elizabeth said. 'And he doubled payments to Mum.'

'You still see him, don't you?' Slim said, turning to Sarah. 'I didn't recognise you at the time, but it was you in that house in Newport wasn't it?'

Sarah opened her mouth and for a moment Slim thought she would deny it. Then she looked down, shaking her head. 'He prefers to pay me in cash if he can. It leaves less of a trail. He owns that house. Usually it's rented out but he's between tenants.'

'Did he warn you about me?'

Sarah sighed. 'He said Georgia was digging around again. He said it might be a good idea if we went away for a couple of weeks. I agreed because that's what he wanted to hear. I had no intention of going anywhere, though.'

'It's not easy for Mum to travel,' Elizabeth said.

Slim looked back at the girl. 'So you pretended to be your own sister? For two years? How on earth did no one notice?'

Elizabeth shrugged. 'All I had to do was keep my mouth shut and play along. I thought it was going to be hard, that I'd get figured out straight away, but I didn't. No one said a word.'

'I told her school she was moving,' Sarah said. 'James provided faked documents from a boarding school in the Midlands.'

'And no one suspected anything?'

Sarah shook her head. 'Everyone was so delighted that Emily Martin was back, that nothing else mattered.'

'And Georgia?'

'James said her medication was increased. She was half out of it, easy to fool. And Elizabeth didn't even have to pretend to like her. She's a teenager after all.'

'This is insane,' Slim said. 'You impersonated your own sister and no one noticed?'

'A few kids at school were suspicious,' Elizabeth said. 'But I just played the amnesia card. I thought it would be difficult, but it wasn't. I just buried my head, got on with taking another girl's exams. That's why I'm going through the motions at night school. Because now I have to take my own.'

'I noticed you weren't trying so hard,' Slim said with a wry smile.

Elizabeth shrugged. 'Why would I? I've already studied it all once.'

'What are you going to do now?' Sarah said, leaning forward, her lower lip trembling with fear.

Slim stood up. 'I'm going to catch a bus,' he said. 'I came here to find Emily Martin, but I didn't find her. I hope you'll both forgive me for the intrusion on your time.'

44

Bernadette kicked at a railing, sending an echoing clang through the deserted park. 'Elizabeth impersonated her sister for nearly two years and no one knew? I can't believe that.'

'No one was looking,' Slim said. 'And the two people who did know—Elizabeth and James—were already familiar with each other. They didn't need to fake their relationship. And Georgia, manipulated by James, was fooled. I checked the medication I found in their house online. Strong antidepressants that would have left her in a fugue-like state. I gather she stopped taking them after Emily—I mean Elizabeth—left, prompting her to contact me.'

'And James, desperate to please her, let her, assuming you wouldn't find anything.'

'He was right. I've uncovered an unholy mess, but I haven't found his daughter. The girl lying by the river that day wasn't Emily at all, but her sister.'

'How could no one notice two girls who looked so similar just one town apart?'

Slim chuckled. 'They went to different schools, had different circles of friends, wore their hair different ... haven't you ever met anyone who so closely resembled you it was frightening?'

Bernadette cocked her head. 'No, I haven't. No surprise there. What about you?'

Slim sighed. 'Only in the mirror after a heavy night. I hope that there's only the one of me to be a burden on the world.'

'I think we could do with a few more,' Bernadette said. 'There are a lot of cold cases.'

'Thanks. I think.'

'And what was it Carter saw? The pram? Who was in it?'

Slim shook his head. 'Nothing. Sometimes after Annabel died, Sarah still went to see Emily. She used the pram as a walker because it made it easier to get across the field. And perhaps, I don't know, on some level maybe it helped her feel she was bringing her daughters together.'

'She sounds like a wacko,' Bernadette said.

'I think most of us would be after everything that happened to her,' Slim said.

Bernadette sighed. 'So what happened to Emily at the end of it all? Do you have any idea? Is she still alive? Still missing?'

Slim shook his head. 'I don't think so,' he said. 'There are two people who know half of the story. The person who abducted Emily, and the person who moved her body.'

'James?'

Slim nodded. 'He knows the second half. He knows where she is. What I need him to do is tell me what he knows of the rest.'

'And will he?'

'Maybe.'

'But he doesn't need to, does he? Because you've already figured it out.'

In the trees, above them, a crow began to caw. To the east the sky was lightening; they had talked all night. Slim stared at the gloom under the trees, wondering how he would ever make his theory stick.

'I might,' he said. 'First, however, I need to make a couple more phone calls.' He smiled. 'Funnily enough, both to teachers. I was never much of one to listen when I was at school, but it's never too late to start, is it?'

45

Kevin Milliner, 22, had died of an overdose, five months before Emily's disappearance. Slim had come across the article by chance when searching online for the medication Georgia Martin had been taking. The drug had been found in the man's blood, likely cut with whatever else he had consumed, a heavy painkiller, able to take the edge off reality. Available only on prescription.

The young man had lived in Liftondown, a couple of miles outside Launceston, and had likely gone to school with Julian Carter, who had supplied him with drugs. Carter, who had been sleeping with a doctor's wife to get his hands on prescription medication, and had somehow encountered Emily Martin during one of his escapades. Emily, whose mother had been on a series of medication for ongoing depression issues, and who had no trouble pilfering a few of her unsuspecting mother's pills.

The picture attached to the article had shown a troubled, drug-addicted young man, his eyebrows tightened above eyes surrounded by age lines that befitted someone far older. Acne likely brought on by substance abuse had left him barely recognisable from the time Slim had seen his picture before.

It was highly probable that Emily and Carter had been sleeping together, the small-town dealer swapping an older model for a much younger one. It would take a confession from Carter to prove, however, and it really didn't matter anyway, when it came down to Emily's abduction. It was only circumstantial.

Grabbing a takeaway coffee from a chain store on Launceston High Street, he walked across to a bench near a tall war memorial and pulled out his phone.

Miss May at Launceston Primary School had already confirmed one of his suspicions, but he had one more he needed to check.

He dialled the number. It rang a couple of times before a man answered.

'Yes?'

'Is that Dave Brockhill? This is, uh, Mike Lewis. From the BBC? I was wondering if I could have a quick talk to you about a couple of your former classmates.'

~

Dartmoor's desolate loveliness maintained its shine despite the heavy thunderclouds in Slim's head as he climbed, close on the trail behind James, whom he had allowed to push ahead. The conversation they needed to have could wait until they'd both had time to enjoy the peak.

They reached the tor they had been heading for half an hour later. Slim sat down on a rock and pulled a flask of coffee out of his bag, perhaps the last one Georgia would ever make for him. Back at the house, he had already packed away his things, and left the suitcase by the door so Georgia could clean his room. He hadn't yet spoken to

James, but he had told Georgia that he planned to close the case, their fee waived. He would never get money out of James anyway, and he would survive, one way or another. He could find a couch somewhere as long as he kept a tab on the drinking, and there would always be another case.

'She liked it up here, didn't she?'

'Who?'

'Emily. Those pictures you showed me. There were three pictures of you and Emily up here. She liked it, didn't she?'

James nodded. 'She liked the open space. We both did. And the fresh air. And it didn't matter up here that she couldn't speak. She could communicate with nature in other ways.' He smiled. 'Our walks together were some of the few times I saw her without her ... anger.'

'It must have been hard, to feel trapped like that.'

'The older she became, the worse it got. Georgia wouldn't let her go to a special school. That didn't help. If she had ... things might have been different.'

Slim looked out at the desolate moor, the rocky hilltops, the grassy valleys with scattered flocks of sheep and wandering moorland ponies. 'It has a certain beauty, doesn't it?' Slim said. 'If I died, I can think of worse places to be buried,' he added, carefully watching James's reaction. 'It's a shame no one would want to carry me up here. They'd probably leave me by the side of the road.'

James stared straight ahead. 'There are worse places,' he said.

'You know, life isn't like a story,' Slim said. 'In a story, I'd either kick the booze and live happily ever, or it'd end me. I'd go down with some stirring last word, there'd be a piano jingle, and the credits would roll. It wouldn't be like this, just on and on, a good day, a bad day. Over and over, this relentless fight to take back control of myself, and the perpetual concern that I might not make it. You know what I mean, don't you?'

James nodded.

'In real life, stories have holes,' Slim continued. 'You don't always find out where a body is buried, or who murdered the kid. You just have a string of events, some that you can understand, some that you can't. People don't always act with organised, cold motives. Sometimes they do something because they're trying to cover a lie and they think that it's the right decision at the time, but in doing so they create a bigger lie, and soon the heap of lies is so big that there's no going back. And sometimes the person building the heap of lies continues to do so until they no longer know why. It becomes a habit like any other.'

James still said nothing. He took a bite out of a chocolate bar and stared straight ahead as a single tear rolled down his cheek.

'I know you didn't murder Emily,' Slim said. 'Why would you have done? She was your daughter. But I know she's dead. The evidence points to her still being missing, but she's not, is she? In all the time we've spent together, you've never once talked about her as though she were still alive, even though I was led to believe she only lived one town over. You've always talked about her as though she were dead, and sometimes, when you mentioned the girl I was led to believe was Emily, I caught a little hesitation on your tongue, as though you were consciously reminding yourself of your daughter's name. It took me a while to understand why, but I figured it out in the end.' He paused to take a sip of coffee, wincing at the satisfying bitterness. It had taken a while, but Georgia was finally making it the way he liked it.

'You didn't kill Emily,' Slim said, 'but I know you

buried her. I won't ask where, not unless you want to tell me. I hope it was somewhere pretty.'

James continued to stare straight ahead. Slim wondered whether over the buffeting wind the man had actually heard. Then, almost too quietly for Slim to hear, James said, 'Near to a river, where we sometimes swam.'

Slim saw the way years of denial and regret suddenly broke through the shield James had maintained for the last two years, and in part for much longer. Slim saw an essentially good man, but one who had made mistakes, and in continuing to correct his mistakes had built a new world for himself, one he barely recognised. As James's face creased, and he covered his mouth, sobbing silently into his hand, Slim looked away, allowing the man a few moments of privacy.

'It was hard enough having to bury your daughter,' he said, 'but you knew there was a way you could avoid Georgia having to do it too. You knew it would hurt, but you weighed things up and you figured it was the lesser of the hurts.'

'It would have destroyed her,' James said, his face in his hands. 'She wanted everything perfect. She always did. We had no idea about Emily's speech problem. Not until it was too late.'

'Too late to swap for the other twin?' Slim said, immediately regretting allowing his personal feelings to intrude on the impartiality he had promised himself to uphold.

'Too late,' James said, the tremble in his voice revealing that he barely held on.

'Because Annabel wasn't enough, was she? You knew there was something wrong with her so the pair of you hatched a plan. Georgia had been working on the pharmacy counter at Treliske Hospital and knew the place inside out. That made it easy.'

Slim waited for James to nod, but instead the older man turned to look at him. 'You don't know everything,' he said. 'You think you've got it all worked out, but you haven't.'

'So enlighten me.'

'Annabel ... she wasn't mine.'

Slim thought of the video taken from Andy's camera, of Graham Reeves' car, of Georgia getting out. He remembered how Reeves had talked about Georgia's postnatal depression, and how he had seemed to know so much more about the woman even than James did. Then there was his wife's death from a heart condition. Something hereditary? The pieces fit. The puzzle wasn't yet complete, and Slim couldn't be sure those pictured even knew they were part of it. But they might. They just might.

'I knew it,' James continued, 'because I wasn't around when she would have been conceived. We were having problems. Georgia was going through one of her bad patches. Sarah offered me a couch for a few days.'

'Where things happened?'

James flapped a hand in frustration. 'At that time I thought it was over with Georgia. I knew Sarah was pregnant, and I was ready to leave Georgia and move in with her. I had the court case coming up, and it looked better for my sentencing if I was happily married. I got out after a few months. I didn't expect to come home to a newborn child.'

'That wasn't yours?'

'No. I know what I did was stupid, but I wasn't thinking straight. Georgia was out cold one night, heavily medicating herself as she often did, so I took the baby and I ... swapped it for one of mine.'

Slim looked down. Waves of sorrow struck him like the bow of a ship. Through everything he'd been through and seen, this was something new. In many ways, something far worse.

'Wouldn't it have been easier just to leave Georgia?'

James closed his eyes. 'I've thought about it a thousand times,' he said. 'Before and since. Of course it would have been. But I didn't. I thought I loved her, despite everything, but maybe it was more than that. Maybe I was trying to minimalise the damage. She's always been a fragile person. I was afraid if I left she might do something stupid.'

'So you stayed. You turned down a chance at happiness with a woman you loved and who had borne you twins to stay with a woman you convinced yourself you loved, and who had given birth to another man's child.'

James grimaced. 'In a nutshell.'

'And to make it a little easier, you make sure at least you'd be bringing up your own child.' Slim couldn't resist a little scoff, although he tried to disguise it as a clearing of his throat. 'One of them, at least.'

'Something like that.'

Slim sighed. 'It might have been easier just to make a choice and let someone down.'

'Isn't life always easier in hindsight?'

'At least we agree on something.'

They both fell silent. Slim watched a herd of moorland ponies moving through the valley below. He opened his flask again and took a last swallow, wishing the liquid was something stronger than coffee.

'There's still the question of Emily,' Slim said. 'You don't know who killed her.'

'There was a note,' James said. 'Sent to an old email, one I hadn't used in years. I'd been filling my time going through old documents to take my mind off things. I almost missed it.' He gave a long, resigned sigh. 'It told me where I'd find her,' he said, his voice tinged with regret. 'All it said was, "It doesn't pay to forget. Go alone." And it had an address. I thought it was a load of rubbish, someone having a laugh, but it was just down the road, so I nipped out to take a look. And there she was. Strangled.'

'You didn't know the sender?'

'It was just a line of numbers. I thought it was spam. I checked the IP address and it came up as nothing. Whoever sent it made sure they couldn't be traced.'

And you didn't tell the police?'

'How could I?'

Slim nodded. 'Pull one thread and the whole sweater unravels.'

James shrugged.

'Would it make a difference if you knew who had done it? Because when everything is said and done, murder is murder.'

James grimaced. 'It might.'

46

Saturday.

Slim stopped by Bernadette's house on the way up to the bus stop. A bedraggled man of about Slim's age answered the door.

'I'm looking for Bernadette,' Slim said.

Without a word the man shrugged, shook his head, then turned and hollered back over his shoulder, before tramping away into the house as Bernadette, in jeans and t-shirt, came to the door.

'Sorry about him,' she said. 'He's not good with mornings.'

Slim had resisted the urge to punch the man, figuring it wouldn't do Bernadette any favours, and the man already looked like his world was on the verge of collapse without any further intervention.

'I came to bring you this,' Slim said, handing over an envelope. 'It's a reference letter with a couple of copies. I hope it helps. If you lose it, or you need more, you'll find a phone number and an email for me inside.' He pulled his ancient, battered Nokia out of his pocket. 'Try the phone first. I couldn't lose this thing if I tried.' He smirked. 'And I did try once.'

'You're leaving?'

Slim nodded. 'I have one last errand to run and then I'm gone. It's time to move on.'

Bernadette stepped out on to the front step and gripped Slim in a tight bear hug.

'I'll miss you,' she said.

'We might see each other again,' he said. 'Particularly if you end up as the copper I think you can be. I'm too skint to give this game up just yet, and no doubt you'll end up pulling me in for some misdemeanour or other.'

Bernadette hugged him one more time, then let go and stepped back with tears in her eyes.

'What about the case?'

Slim smiled. 'You'll read about it in the papers,' he said. 'And if you don't, then just assume I got it wrong. Goodbye, Bernadette. And good luck.' Then, thinking about Alan Coaker's certain reaction, he added, 'Keep the taser. Just in case.'

'Thanks. Goodbye, Slim.'

He turned and walked away. He hated the whole lingering goodbye thing, so at the bottom of the path he turned and waved her back inside. Reluctantly she went, but as he reached the end of the street and took one last glance back, he saw she had come back outside. He lifted a hand and waved, then walked quickly around the corner, leaving her behind.

He had memorised the bus timetable and had to hurry. He was made to rush further by a need to stop by the police station and drop a thick envelope of his findings through the post box. He hesitated only a moment, feeling a brief pang of guilt, but for all of James's attempts to balance his life, despite the corrosion happening at both ends, murder was murder. And justified or not, a teenage girl had still been killed in cold blood.

Only when he reached the bus station did he realize he had nowhere in particular to go after his last errand. Still, he could mull that over later.

Wondering whether he should try to resurrect his old business or perhaps change careers altogether, he looked up as a bus bound for Plymouth pulled in.

∽

He remembered the way from his previous visit. She frowned when she opened the door, cocking her head to one side as though she thought he was a traveller who had lost his way.

'Hello again,' she said. 'Mike, isn't it?'

'Hello, Norah. Sure, Mike is fine. Can I come in? There's something I want to talk to you about.'

'Well, I suppose.'

She stepped back to allow him to enter.

'I just wanted to thank you,' he said. 'The information you provided about your aunt and the Woodland Man proved very interesting. There's definitely the potential for a TV documentary there. And I also wanted to say I'm so very sorry, about what happened both to your son ... and to your best friend.'

Norah had been about to take a seat, but now she stepped back. 'What?'

'Kevin Milliner. Your son. He kept your married name, before you divorced. It wasn't hard for me to find out. I mean, you have his picture over there on your mantelpiece. He must have fallen on hard times since then, but still, it's clearly the same person whose picture I found online.'

'If this is for another of your documentaries, you can forget it.'

Slim lifted a hand. 'It's not. I'm sorry for your loss. I really am.'

'Well, that's nice of you to say—'

'Not just your son, either. Your best friend.'

'Who?'

Slim took a deep breath, brushing sentimentality aside. Sometimes he had to be the detective shielding the fragilities of the man, adopt a hard exterior, and go for the jugular before his target had time to pull out of the way.

'Susan Cole-Bridger. The one they called Smelly Sue. I saw you in some old class photographs. Standing next to each other, best friends.'

Now Norah slumped down into an armchair. 'How could you know?'

Slim remained standing. 'I made a couple of phone calls that only confirmed what I had thought. It left you heartbroken, didn't it? But you knew, didn't you? Who put the dead bird in her locker. Did she tell you … before she died?'

Norah narrowed her eyes. 'She left her diary in my art folder,' she said. 'I didn't find it until two days after her death.'

'And you were angry. You let it smoulder all these years. You'd always hoped to get payback against James Martin.'

'Not James,' Norah said, her eyes glazed, not looking up. 'Georgia.'

'Huh.' Slim lifted an eyebrow. So, James had dropped another lie. He hadn't been checking his emails, but Georgia's. Perhaps he had known she had rekindled her relationship with Graham Reeves, and been trying to catch her out. Or perhaps not. He might never know.

'She was always so full of herself,' Norah said, her tone

biting, looking away as she idly tugged at a loose thread pulled out of the armchair's upholstery. 'The perfect girl, the one all the boys wanted. And she used to rip on Sue for every little thing. Even before what happened, I *hated* her.'

'It's nice to get something wrong,' Slim said. 'But you still have plenty of motive.'

Norah looked up, frowning. 'What are you talking about? Who are you?'

In the distance, Slim heard the faint peal of a siren. Norah, facing him, hands clasped over her stomach, didn't seem to have noticed.

'She trusted you.'

'Who?'

'Emily Martin. You were her teacher at Launceston Art Club. I didn't recognise you at first in the newspaper's photograph because the quality was so poor, and of course because they incorrectly labelled you as Mrs. Miller. However, I know you worked in the primary school on Wednesday mornings because I called Miss May last night to make sure. Emily wasn't feeling well but was walking over to see you that day, perhaps to meet you after lunch.'

Slim remembered the camera footage. The car reversing. The same car that was currently parked outside Norah's house.

'She saw her mother with another man, and she panicked. She went across the sports fields to the school, and saw you outside, just as you were getting ready to leave. She went back to check on her mother, and you came and picked her up. You drove back past her house to pick up her phone, which she wasn't allowed in school due to a school rule, then you made her switch it off so her parents couldn't trace her.'

'This is all just—'

Slim lifted his voice, drowning out her protests. 'She

wanted to stay with you, but you never really felt the same way she did. Your son had only recently died, and you could trace the path of what had killed him back to Emily Martin because she had confided certain things in you. You blamed her for his death, and here she was, wanting to hide out at your house. And the anniversary of your best friend's suicide was quickly approaching. I saw a bunch of dead flowers in a jar down by the tree Sue hung herself from. They were the same flowers as those dried ones you've got over there in a vase. It's you that puts them there every year, isn't it?'

Norah was shaking her head, but it was more in wonderment than denial. The sirens were louder now, but Norah still appeared not to hear.

'You're crazy,' she said at last.

Slim wasn't done. He wanted to hear her say the words. As Norah leaned forward, her head in her hands, he squatted down beside the chair.

'Even then, after everything, you might not have hurt Emily. You're not a natural killer, I can tell. Not someone who's done it before. Yet you have strong hands from working with sculpture, and it's not like anyone would hear Emily cry out, even if she could. Perhaps you were showing her your studio in one of those outbuildings? They're built pretty solid. I mean, you can barely hear the canaries in the aviary up there. I wouldn't have guessed they were there until I saw the bags of feed over there by the door.'

Norah started to get up. 'I want you to leave,' she said, but her voice was hollow, her resilience fading.

'I think she stayed here a while,' Slim continued. 'It's a big enough property. You could have easily hidden her if the police came knocking. But she got under your skin, didn't she, and on the eight day, the exact length of time

Eight Days

poor Susan suffered before she went down into the woods, you were tense. Perhaps Emily said something wrong, and you lost control. And then, faced with a body, you decided to leave her where Sue had died.'

Norah stared at him. Her mouth moved, but no words came out.

Slim couldn't resist a grim smile. 'When I saw you try to kick that cat, I guessed you might have a temper. And a cruel streak, too, perhaps. After all, the bird they found had its feet taped to the tree branch, so tightly one of its legs had broken. Cruel, but artistic in a certain way, wasn't it? And it certainly deflected attention.' He sighed. 'You could have left it there, but you couldn't resist sending an anonymous email to Georgia, hoping she would find the body. Unfortunately, Georgia's health hasn't been the best, and James has a tendency to pry. Even so, the stars aligned pretty well.' Slim shrugged. 'It must have been a real shock to read about her recovery.'

Norah frowned. 'I was certain she was dead,' she said, and Slim, feeling the wire brushing against the inside of his shirt—another loan from Alan—felt a little leap of elation at getting the confession at last. 'She was cold, but the news said ... and I thought, I've been given a second chance. I did something terrible, but I was forgiven.'

Slim shook his head. 'Unfortunately not,' he said. 'Emily Martin—the real Emily Martin—died.'

The sirens were right outside. Norah finally seemed to notice them. She looked around as though for a weapon, then stared at the front door as a heavy knock was accompanied by a shout of 'Open up, please.'

Slim sighed. As Norah jumped up from the chair and began to rush back and forth, he glanced over his shoulder at the bay window, at the view of the fields and the valley. He caught a glimpse of flickering lights through the trees, another police car on a lane behind the property, blocking off any escape route.

Things would change, they had to. But when everything was said and done, after families had been pulled apart and perhaps in some cases reunited, the wind would still whistle through the grass, and ruffle through the trees.

END

ABOUT THE AUTHOR

Jack Benton is a pen name of Chris Ward, the critically acclaimed author of the dystopian *Tube Riders* series, the horror/science fiction *Tales of Crow* series, and the *Endinfinium* YA fantasy series, as well as numerous other well-received stand alone novels.

Eight Days is the sixth volume in the Slim Hardy Mystery Series.

There will be more.

Chris would love to hear from you:

www.amillionmilesfromanywhere.net/tokyolost

chrisward@amillionmilesfromanywhere.net

ACKNOWLEDGMENTS

Thanks to my regular contributors, Elizabeth for the cover, Nick for the proofreading, and the incomparable Jenny Avery for the fact checking and invaluable knowledge of pretty much everything. In addition, many thanks as always to my muses Jenny Twist and John Daulton, as well as to my wonderful Patreon supporters:

Alan McDonald
Janet Hodgson
Ken Gladwin
Rosemary Kenny
Sean Flanagan
Jane Ornelas
Gail Beth La Vine
Anja Peerdeman
Betty Martin
Katherine Crispin
Jenny Brown
Eda Ridgway
Sharon Kenneson

Leigh McEwan
Amaranth Dawe
Nancy
Ron

You guys are fantastic and your support means so much.
   Happy reading,
   JB

Printed in Great Britain
by Amazon